From the first paragraph, the very first sentence, Murali Kamma had me engrossed and engaged in the narrative, and my interest did not diminish until I got to end of the book, twenty stories in all, to its very last sentence. Understated and unpretentious, this is a remarkable debut collection, that does not attempt to shock or surprise by "gross and violent stimulants," but relies on depicting plainly the life and situations that ordinary people face in their lives, and so it reaches out in ways that are likely to have a deeper and more lasting effect on readers than mere sensationalized subject or a dazzling surface experimentation with words and styles are likely to do. It catches people in the flow of their lives, as thinking, feeling, quietly struggling persons, dealing with life's constraints, conventions, and demands and to find for themselves the space and opportunity to gain just that bit of illumination, momentary though it may be, that may make sense of all the endeavor and aspiration that marks a human's trajectory on earth—the negotiating of familial relationships, the displacements in and of cultures and locales, the accidental encounters, the charting of a path, itself somewhat casual and fortuitous, toward a transient gleam of the self, of goodness and courtesy, before moving along on the journey. There is sorrow here, and pain, unslaked longing, crises of faith, socially-conditioned prejudice and obligation, and the small, quiet ways in which all this is dealt with, steadily opposed, and checked without fuss, not, though, without the recognition of the more strident struggles and protests in the background. And the stories eschew the conclusive, neatly tied endings, working more through suggestion and the opening up of possibility than by imposing a (forced) denouement. Rich, silted, streams and currents from the vast river that is life, *Not Native* is a book to treasure for its deep wisdom and exquisite feeling in their ripple, swirl, and flow.

—**Waqas Khwaja**, Ellen Douglass Leyburn Professor of English, Agnes Scott College, author *Hold Your Breath* and *No One Waits for the Train*

In this exciting and moving debut collection, Murali Kamma explores the immigrant condition with compassion and candor. Readers, no matter what their background, will relate to these characters who are part Indian, part American, and wholly human.
—**Chitra Banerjee Divakaruni**, author of *Before We Visit the Goddess* and *The Forest of Enchantments*

A fresh, engaging collection from an excellent writer of short fiction. Most of us in this country came originally from different places—geographically, socially, and spiritually. And while bodies can be easily transported, it takes longer for uprooted spirits to engage the new territory. Once arrived, each successive generation must deal with the ongoing consequences of that journey, and the changes it brings into their lives. In each of these tales, Murali Kamma engages the past and present dimensions of that struggle, illuminating, along the way, what it means to be Indian, American, and truly human.
—**Roderick Clark**, Editor/Publisher of *Rosebud* magazine

A collection of powerful stories that opens up a larger world for the reader. The haunting quality and the emotional punch they deliver linger in the mind. This is a writer to watch.
—**Bharti Kirchner**, author of *Darjeeling, Goddess of Fire*, and *Season of Sacrifice*

NOT NATIVE

Short Stories of Immigrant Life in an In-Between World

NOT NATIVE

Short Stories of Immigrant Life in an In-Between World

Murali Kamma

Wising Up Press Collective
Wising Up Press

Wising Up Press
P.O. Box 2122
Decatur, GA 30031-2122
www.universaltable.org

Catalogue-in-Publication data is on file with the Library of Congress.
LCCN: 2019940118

Wising Up ISBN: 978-1-7324514-3-8

CONTENTS

SONS AND FATHERS

ON DISTANT SHORES

SCHISMS AND SURPRISES

AT CROSS PURPOSES

To

Anandhi and Amit

for always being there and for making it all possible

it is not native here
that may be the one
thing we are sure of
it came from somewhere
else perhaps alone
—W. S. Merwin ("Unknown Bird")

The first sentence was true. The second was invention. But together—to me, the writer—they had done something extraordinary.

—V. S. Naipaul ("Prologue to an Autobiography")

It looked as though he wanted to tell some story.

—Anton Chekhov ("About Love")

SONS AND FATHERS

THE END OF THE ROAD

When the express train pulled into the station, its wheels screeching in protest, Giri's father stood up and said he was going to buy some bananas. It wasn't a long stop, so Giri's mother told him to be careful and not go far from their coach. "Don't worry" were his last words before he stepped onto the platform and disappeared into a crowd of hurrying and arriving passengers, red-uniformed porters carrying suitcases, relatives saying goodbye or hello, and vendors crying, "Chai . . . coffee . . . chai!" She never saw him again.

At first, as the train started moving again and he didn't show up, she thought he was in another coach. Perhaps there hadn't been enough time to get back. But when the train, having left the station, gathered speed, she became agitated and wondered aloud whether she should pull the chain. A co-passenger cautioned her, saying that she'd get penalized if it wasn't an emergency. No need to worry, he added soothingly, because he hadn't seen her husband linger at the fruit stall. There were no corridor connections, so he must be stuck in another coach. When the train made another stop, hours later, and there was still no sign of her husband, the co-passenger, his face red with embarrassment, offered his apologies and went to look for the train conductor. The conductor who came over was sympathetic, but he said there was little he could do at this point. If her husband remained missing, she'd have to contact the police.

Giri was waiting on the platform with his grandfather to receive his parents—although only his mother, of course, her face somber, got down from the train and told them why her husband wasn't there. By now she was not only worried but furious as well. He'd deceived her. Despite his assurances and calm demeanor, she realized that Giri's father hadn't taken his pills for a couple of days.

At home, after giving him his pills every day, she'd wait until he swallowed them—and though he protested sometimes, darkly grumbling that he was being poisoned, she never let him skip his dose. Without the pills, she reminded him, he'd end up in an institution. And it always worked. On the train, however, she didn't want to make a fuss in front of the other passengers, especially since he was in a good mood. Sitting on the upper berth, with an open magazine beside him, he'd asked for his pill bottle and even poured himself a cup of water. But that had been a ruse. Later, counting the pills in the bottle, she discovered that he'd fooled her. The following morning, oddly enough, he appeared fine as he sat next to a barred window, holding the same magazine, and watched the sparsely populated, sunbaked countryside whiz by. True, he was unusually subdued. But she thought it was because, like her, he hadn't slept well. The coffee revived her, and she thought he'd also perked up after their upma and omelet breakfast, which they'd bought from a vendor. So when he got off with only his wallet, saying that he wanted to buy bananas, she thought nothing of it.

Giri's grandfather said they should wait, even after the train left. They scanned the faces of exiting passengers, checked the waiting room, and went to the station manager's office to make inquiries. But it all seemed pointless. "Let's go," he finally said, looking grim.

Once they got home, he took charge of things in his usual forthright manner. Giri and his mother were his responsibility from now on, he said. In fact, Giri was already living with his grandparents. He'd been sent there about a year earlier, at the insistence of his grandfather, who thought he shouldn't be living with his parents when his father was ill. The patriarch controlled his extended family with an iron hand—and while nobody had the temerity to challenge him, Giri was happy because he liked his grandparents and the new school he attended.

When Giri's father had lost his job, diminishing the family's prospects and creating anxiety, the old man had agreed to help them financially—but on one condition. What Giri's father needed, he said, was the attention of a well-qualified specialist who had just returned from abroad. He was highly recommended, and thanks to a mutual friend, getting a consultation with him wouldn't be difficult. A battery of tests would be needed, he added, to figure out the best way forward. Giri's father agreed, or at least that's what they thought.

So where did he go? An accident was ruled out—they would have heard about it by now, surely. Assembling his relatives, Giri's grandfather decided to dispatch a search party. He also filed a police report. But that didn't fill him with confidence, even though there were few other options in the pre-internet, pre-cellphone era—because the police were understaffed and underpaid, not to mention overwhelmed with cases higher on their priority list. For the all-male search party, without any leads or luck, the task proved to be hopeless. Carrying his photo, they visited hotels and lodges, talked to vendors in and around the train station, and questioned autorickshaw and cab drivers. They even distributed fliers and placed a notice in the local newspaper. Giri's father, however, had vanished without leaving a trace.

Standing in the doorway of his train as it grinds to a halt, Giri watches the hustle and bustle on the platform, wondering how much things have changed since his father disembarked here all those years ago. The city would have greatly altered. Nevertheless, though Giri lives in the U.S. now, he knows his native country well enough to realize that much would also be the same. The station, for instance, may be bigger and more modern-looking, with the train timings displayed electronically on sleek terminals, but it still looks chaotic. He hears a familiar chant—"Chai . . . coffee . . . chai!"—and the loudspeakers crackle as the train's arrival is announced in three languages. The red-uniformed porters swiftly approach the dark blue coaches, seeking customers, while the relatives waiting on the platform look for their loved ones.

This side trip wasn't something he'd planned in advance. Giri had been coming to India—as he did almost every year, even if the visit was brief—to spend time with his mother. But this time there was a surprise. Actually, it came as a shock. His mother, smiling nervously, announced that she was getting married again; she hadn't mentioned it earlier because she was waiting to see Giri. Things had moved quickly, she said, and until the divorce papers arrived, she wasn't sure it was going to happen. Then she had another surprise. Handing Giri a neatly folded sheet of paper, she said, "You should go and see him . . . he asked about you."

There is nobody at the station to receive Giri. He has come alone, and he will leave alone. His mother's wedding is about ten days away—but since she didn't need his help, saying that they were keeping it very simple, he decided to make this trip. Getting off the train, Giri accepts a porter's offer to carry his bag, even though it's small. Not having booked a hotel room, he was planning to do it online during the journey. But he barely glanced at his cellphone.

Giri's co-passenger turned out to be a friendly Sikh businessman who kept him entertained with his banter, and he recommended a comfortable hotel near the station.

Emerging from the imposing, noisy building with other passengers, Giri pays the porter and makes his way to the hotel, which is in a lane just off the congested main road going past the station. The hotel is undergoing renovation, judging by the scaffolding, but inside it is fine, even elegant in an old-fashioned and understated way. The revolving ceiling fans in the lobby catch his attention, as does the absence of any computers. "They're being installed, sir," says an employee at the check-in desk, with a sheepish smile, as he jots down Giri's personal details in a book.

Waiting for his room key, Giri notices a framed picture on the wall behind the desk. The picture was taken, according to the caption, on the day of the hotel's inauguration. Looking at the date, he realizes with a shock that it opened in the year his father chose this city for his disappearing act. No way he could have stayed here, of course, since the hotel had opened about two months after his father's arrival. Still, the coincidence is striking. A few smiling people are in the blown-up picture—and while the hotel behind them looks much the same, the land next to it is mostly vacant. Not anymore. The area surrounding the hotel is totally built up and teeming with life, no doubt because the station has grown in importance as a rail hub.

Pushing the hotel door open to step outside, about an hour later, Giri feels the humidity hit him on the face like a wet towel. Then there's the dust and the din of honking vehicles on the main road, where a couple of policemen, wearing masks, are directing the endless traffic with calm determination. The first person to approach Giri is a cab driver, who, having just dropped off a passenger at the hotel, asks him if he needs to go anywhere.

"Yes," says Giri, who has already showered and eaten a light meal that he ordered from his room. Taking out the paper his mother had given him, he unfolds it and reads the address.

The driver seems puzzled for a moment, but then his face brightens. "Oh, yes, it's in the old city," he says. "I haven't been there in a while. I can take you, but I'll have to drop you off where the road ends."

"What do you mean?"

"There's a path that goes to the top, but it's only for pedestrians. It's not long. My cab cannot go beyond the bottom of the hill. The road ends there."

"Sure," Giri says, opening the door to get in. "That's not a problem. I can walk."

After her husband vanished, Giri's mother remained with her father and helped him in his business. He was a wholesale clothing merchant who even had overseas clients. As she got more comfortable in her role as a businesswoman, her father scaled back his involvement and eventually retired. When Giri's grandmother died, his mother took over the household responsibilities as well, and the three of them lived peacefully and comfortably, until another crisis threatened to disrupt their lives.

Giri's mother reconnected with a childhood friend, and they fell in love. To get married again, she'd have to divorce her husband first. But how was that going to happen if they didn't know where Giri's father lived, assuming he was still alive? Giri's grandfather, when he found out about his daughter's love interest, was surprisingly open about it. He was an unusual man, a man whose background and age hadn't stopped him from being ahead of his time.

But for Giri, who was in high school by then, it was a difficult time. The situation was highly awkward and he dreaded any fallout. He found it embarrassing, but at the same time he wanted his mother to be happy. Fortunately, his mother's lover was pleasant and Giri got along well with him. They were discreet—but more important, so were the handful of people who knew about the relationship.

Giri was nonetheless glad to escape when a well-known university, hundreds of miles away, offered a scholarship. His grandfather died that year, and Giri's mother shut down the business shortly afterwards. She and her beau moved to a big city, also hundreds of miles away and where they didn't know anybody, and began a new life together. Giri stayed in touch with his mother and visited them on his breaks. When he said that he was hoping to go abroad for higher studies, if he could get financial assistance, they encouraged him. So that's how Giri ended up in the U.S., where he remained—and became a naturalized citizen—after getting married to a local fellow graduate student at his university.

"This is where we stop," the cab driver says, pulling over. "You get off here."

Stepping out after paying the fare, Giri sees an unpaved path—wide enough for motorcycles but not cars—snaking up to the top of a hill, where a brick-colored building is partially visible between what look like mahogany trees. A car is parked in a patch of dirt land next to the road, which doesn't go any further. When Giri reaches the path's end, he sees a large grass-covered field ringed by hedges and tall trees, with no other route to the secluded property. Do they use two-wheelers to bring up supplies? There are actually four brick-colored buildings, neatly spaced out and of varying sizes, and they all have identical roofs that look like pyramids. It's eerily quiet with nobody outside, and he doesn't see any signs on the property. Walking past a stone bench and a flowerbed that's ablaze with marigolds, hibiscus and chrysanthemums, Giri stops at the building closest to him. The door is wide open, to his surprise. He walks in.

It's cool inside and dimly lit, making him blink as he looks around. When his eyes adjust to the light, he realizes that the anteroom is unoccupied, though he hears low voices. Giri coughs. The murmuring stops, a chair is pushed back—and a door opens, revealing a white-haired man in a grey kurta. Giri gasps, feeling a chill shoot down his spine. Despite the passage of time and a longish beard that partly obscures the man's gaunt face, Giri recognizes him immediately.

"I . . . I'm a visitor," he manages to say. "I just have a few questions."

"Please have a seat," the man says, pointing at a metal chair facing a desk. Then, without showing any sign that he knows who Giri is, the man steps back into the larger room. But he doesn't shut the door—for the consultation, if that's what it was, is over. Following an exchange of goodbyes, a youngish couple emerge from the room and, with scarcely a glance at Giri, quickly exit the building.

"What can I do . . . ?" the man says, coming closer. Then, looking stunned, he stops and stares at him. "My god, I can't believe it! What a surprise . . . and pleasure. Giri?"

"Yes. How are you, Papa? It's been a long time." Giri feels awkward, self-conscious, as if he's talking to a stranger. A memory comes back to him: his father, in the grip of illness, is shaking a fist as he quarrels with Giri's mother. "How do I know he's my son?" he shouts, his eyes blazing.

"I'm doing okay for my age, or at least that's what I think," Giri's father says, smiling. "But look at you! You look wonderful . . . all grown up and handsome. I've heard about your life abroad, and your great job. And I know that you're married. I'm sure your mother is proud of you. I am, though I wasn't involved in any way. Let's step outside. We can sit there and talk in peace. Then I'll show you around."

As they walk up to the stone bench, the memory of another long-ago incident bubbles to the surface. Not long after Giri went to live with his grandparents, he got a visitor at his new school one day. He'd already made friends and was enjoying the school, glad to be away from the uncertainty of his old life. He didn't miss the daily drama at his parents' home, and relished the stability his grandparents provided. He and his classmates were busy talking that day, as they waited for their teacher, when the principal walked in unexpectedly. A hush fell over the room. She was accompanied by their teacher, who called the class to attention and asked Giri to step forward. His heart beating rapidly, he stood up and walked to where they were standing. The principal smiled and, holding his arm, gently led him outside.

"Giri, your father is here," she said. "He's sitting in my office."

"My father is here?" he said uncomprehendingly, as if she'd asked him to repeat after her. "What does he want?"

"He wants to see you. Your grandfather has told me about him. I'll be with you, so there's no need to worry. But you don't have to see him now if you're not keen. It's up to you."

Giri hesitated, but only for a moment. "I don't want to see him now," he said firmly.

"I understand," the principal said, nodding. "You can go back to your seat."

So had he, Giri wonders as he sits on the stone bench, made it easier for his father to leave the family? His father, who has been limping a little, leans back and turns his face towards the sunlight, closing his eyes for a moment. Looking at him again, Giri becomes conscious of his frailty. His teeth are uneven, stained yellow—and while there are no holy markings on his body, a necklace made of beads caresses his chest. He looks like an ascetic. Feeling guilty, Giri looks away. His father seems so different, so vulnerable. Why dredge up those unpleasant memories? And why has he come to see him? Well, how could he not once they knew where he lived? Besides, Giri's father had asked for his U.S. address and was planning to write to him, according to his mother. He'd been pleased to hear that Giri was doing so well. "Give him my address," his father had written in the letter he sent with the divorce papers.

While one mystery—his father's whereabouts—had finally been solved,

Giri's mother hadn't shown interest in knowing more. He got the impression that, having moved on with her life, she didn't want to look back anymore. But Giri is curious.

They sit in silence for a few moments. Gazing in the distance, Giri notices a sudden disturbance as a flock of bright-crested birds, escaping from tall trees like the discharge of a canon, soar into the sky with high-pitched squeals. Bulbuls, most likely. Not far from the stone bench, the blooming flame-of-the-forest tress look as if they're on fire. The hum of traffic, coming from a road that's out of sight, is so faint that it's hard to believe they're in a city.

"Tell me," Giri's father says, turning to him. "Do you know how your mother found me?"

"Yes, you wrote to her after your guru died. But why did you wait that long?"

"Because, Giri, I was scared. My guru didn't know that I had left my family before coming here. I was too embarrassed to tell him. And I didn't want to be kicked out."

Giri wants to ask his father how he met the guru. And why did he choose to abandon his wife and son? But he hesitates to reopen old wounds in the limited time he has here. Amazingly, his father appears normal.

"I don't take meds . . . stopped taking them a long time ago," he says, startling Giri. "I don't need them." He seems to have anticipated his question, although it's a question that Giri had no intention of saying aloud.

"I'm happy to hear that," Giri says. "So you feel okay these days?"

"Yes, I do, except old age is no fun." He laughs. There's no mirth in his eyes, but they shine brightly. "Honestly, I have no major complaints . . . I'm at peace with myself. I stay busy here, even giving advice to people, as you saw. But I still feel bad about what happened, and I hope your mother has forgiven me. I signed the divorce papers, though it took a long time. As for you . . . what can I say? What I did was inexcusable. My only explanation, and it's not a justification, is my illness—"

"They were trying to help you, weren't they? Grandpa was—"

"You're right, Giri." He pauses and looks towards the laterite path, as if he's expecting to see somebody. But there's nobody there and Giri wonders who else is at the ashram at this time. "The plan your grandfather had in mind for me wasn't something I wanted," he continues. "Having agreed reluctantly, I was looking for a way out. Then I saw the magazine article that brought me here."

"You mean there was an article about this ashram?"

"Yes, although the article was really about the guru who founded the ashram. My guru. I knew I had to see him as soon as I read the article. In my bones, I knew he had the solution for me, but I also knew that I had to see him secretly. And urgently. I didn't want any skeptics to dissuade me. As it so happened, we were not far from the ashram. So when the train stopped at the station, I felt compelled to get off."

Giri is astonished. "So you thought coming here without telling anybody would cure you, solve your problem?" he says. "Would Ma have prevented you, even if she didn't share your belief? She became sick with worry, and it destroyed . . . " Giri stops himself from saying more. His intention had been to listen, without becoming critical or emotional, but he lost control.

Giri's father, becoming quiet again, bows his head—and when he clutches his hands, leaning forward, it looks as if he's praying. But his lips aren't moving.

"I made mistakes, big mistakes . . . I don't deny that," he says softly. "My guru is gone, and the ashram is no longer what it was. We'll manage. You may think it's mumbo-jumbo. That's fine. I don't blame you. Even I could scarcely believe that I got saved. Am I delusional? Maybe so, but the fact remains that I've never felt more sane in my life."

Giri remains silent.

Turning to him, his father places a bony hand on his shoulder. "Believe me, son," he says. His other hand trembles and, again, there's a strange glow in his eyes. "For me, it came down to the asylum or the ashram. I chose the ashram."

It sounds pat, almost like a punch line, and Giri wonders if his father rehearsed it in his mind. Then, feeling awful about having such thoughts, he stays quiet. Despite his eagerness to know more, Giri almost didn't come here, afraid of what he'd find and how his father would receive him. Neither he nor his mother had informed him about his visit. Giri didn't see the need. And now, looking at him, Giri doesn't feel the need to question him further—except perhaps to ask if he could spend more time at the place that his father calls home.

ASHES

After Ajay had a late dinner, the driver of the rented car picked him up and they drove for much of the night, stopping once to water the bushes and get chai from a brightly lit roadside eatery that stayed open for truckers. Keen to stay awake during the journey, Ajay sat in the front. He needn't have worried—Ganesh, the driver, played loud Bollywood songs on his CD player, nonstop. The traffic was still sparse when they veered off the highway and took a side road leading to the banks of the Krishna, which at this still hour, as the river flowed unthreateningly, only had a wavering moon for illumination.

The village hadn't awakened—not even a tea stall beckoned—and the rubbish-strewn parking lot they pulled into was deserted, except for a couple of stray dogs that watched the car warily. Ganesh got out and lit a cigarette. Ajay pushed the seat back and dozed, but not for long. Stepping out, he stretched and joined Ganesh; shortly afterwards, they set off down the path that took them to the steps of the riverbank. In a little while, the parking lot would start filling up with vehicles carrying people eager to visit the nearby temple and perhaps take a dip in the river. But Ajay hadn't come as a pilgrim or a tourist; his mission was to immerse his father's ashes in the river. Streaks of orange and red began to appear in the steel grey sky, from where the pumpkin-like moon had disappeared, as they stood gazing at the dark churning water below.

"The priest will be coming from there, sar," Ganesh said, pointing at a cluster of modest houses. "Want chai?"

"Yes!" Ajay walked with Ganesh to a dimly lit shack—and though he had misgivings when he saw an old man getting water from a pump close by, the promise of a hot fragrant brew that was also caffeinated and sweetened lifted his spirits. The water was boiled, after all.

"You've become a stranger to me," his mother had said. "I don't understand you."

The call from India had come a week ago, just as Ajay was returning home after a late day at the office. Their father was dying, his sister said, so he should come quickly. That his father's condition had deteriorated didn't come as a surprise; nevertheless, as he sat in his car, tightly gripping the steering wheel with one hand and his cellphone with the other, it felt strange to be halfway around the world from the hospital room where his mother and sister kept a vigil.

Ajay had been to that hospital over a year ago, soon after their father suffered a stroke. His sister Kavita, whom he called Akka, had also made the trip to India. While she'd stayed back to help their mother take care of him, Ajay hadn't been able to go back since then, even after his mother hinted a couple of times that he should return and relieve his sister.

"Why don't we put him in a nursing home, Amma," he'd said. "That would be better . . . for all of us. They'll take good care of Nana. We can send money from here."

That's when she'd made that statement expressing her bafflement. She couldn't understand him anymore.

But he could understand her. Ajay's visits had become infrequent over the past decade—and though he stayed in touch with his mother, he hadn't spoken to his father in recent years. Ajay's "lifestyle," as his father put it, which involved long-term relationships but no marriage, had been one reason for the rift. Even as a boy in India, Ajay hadn't been close to his father, whose expectations he could never hope to meet. Ajay adored Kavita, his only sibling and a brilliant student who—as the "son" he couldn't be—won a scholarship to the U.S., where she became a scientist and launched a company, paving the way for Ajay's own migration.

Ajay was ecstatic when he got his green card. Tired of being a disappointment to his father, he was glad to escape. It turned out to be a good move. His talents were relatively modest, but Ajay knew he could carve out a decent life if he applied himself—which he did. His passage to America, though, came at a price. He'd become a stranger to his mother as well.

The phone crackled and Ajay lost the connection to India. Instead of dialing, he put the phone down and kept driving, because he wanted to get out of the car first. And he needed time to think. Reaching home, Ajay parked in the garage and went to the kitchen, where he switched on the light and poured himself a glass of cold water. Then he went to the living room. Nana was expected to die soon, so he should come home and—as the only son—be prepared to do the funeral rites, his sister had said. I'm agnostic and don't believe in these rites, Ajay had wanted to say. But he knew that would be an absurd, pompous response. Besides, the rites would be for his father's (and mother's) sake, not his. Picking up the phone, Ajay crashed on the sofa.

Kavita answered. "Amma is upset right now," she said, lowering her voice. "The end is near."

"So sorry I couldn't be there, Akka. It's a difficult time. I'm going to book my ticket now, but please don't wait for me if I get there too late. For the funeral rites, I mean."

"What are you saying, Ajay? You have to be here before we do anything, before we perform any rites. You are the son."

"Akka, I barely spoke to him for several years. And even before that we didn't have a happy relationship. I think it's only right that you should be involved. Also, you are older. I can't believe that in the twenty-first century a woman cannot do her father's last rites."

"Don't talk like that, Ajay. He's your Nana, too. Come quickly. He asked about you the other day and wanted to know when you were coming." Her voice breaking, Kavita hung up.

Ajay didn't speak to his mother, but he imagined her saying: *"You've become a stranger to me. I don't understand you."*

Sitting on a bench outside the shack, Ajay and Ganesh drank large cups of strong tea. It revived Ajay, preparing him for the task ahead. He gave a twenty-rupee note to the old man, who smiled and nodded before informing them that one or two priests should be on the riverbank by now, ready to perform the last rites. There was more daylight now, with deeper hues brightening the sky, as Ajay and Ganesh walked towards the river again. The handful of stalls bordering the path had opened for business, selling water, snacks, and ceremonial items like flowers, incense sticks, camphor, banana leaves, rice and milk. What had been a sleeping village would presently become a gently humming marketplace of visitors, worshippers, vendors and mendicants.

Spotting a priest on the path, they hurried forward to catch him before he started the first ceremony.

"Yes, yes, come there," the priest said, pointing at a small tent on the riverbank. "Bring the ashes, your clothes and the puja items. You can be next."

Then, adjusting the shawl around his shoulders, he turned and went down the steps. Ajay watched him approach a waiting family near the tent. The temple bells pealed and a devotional song unfurled from hidden speakers and floated above the river, where some morning bathers—their eyes closed and lips moving in silent prayer—stood in shallow water and, with folded hands, presented upturned faces to the warming rays of the sun.

"Come, sar, let's go to the car," Ganesh said. The parking lot was about a quarter filled with vans, cars, even autorickshaws. Ajay was about to ask him to open the trunk of the car, when he realized with a start that it was already open.

"*Array*, didn't we close this, sar?"

"Well, I thought I'd closed it, but I'm not sure now," Ajay said. "Maybe I didn't shut it properly."

After his failed attempt to sleep properly in the car, Ajay had asked Ganesh to open the trunk so that he could get the bottle of water he'd bought at the eatery to clean his face and rinse his mouth. He hadn't paid attention to the bag containing his father's ashes and the puja items. Now, with a sickening feeling, Ajay realized the bag was gone. "Who would take it? This is shocking."

"Not shocking, unfortunately," Ganesh said. "You'll find thieves even in these places. But don't blame yourself, sar. It's possible that somebody opened the dickey after we left."

Ajay wasn't sure about that. More likely, he had left it open, tempting somebody who happened to see the bag. Still. Before grabbing it, didn't the person realize he'd be taking stuff that was of value only to the owner? Ajay was puzzled and angry. Just a few minutes earlier, touched by the sun-dappled majesty of the river and the mellifluous song undulating above the heads of worshippers, he was feeling good about the place. And now? Now he felt as if he were in a den of thieves. He couldn't wait to leave. How would his mother and sister react when they found out he'd lost the ashes? The thought filled him with dread.

"What do we do now?" he said, turning to Ganesh. Stunned, he couldn't think straight.

Ganesh didn't answer. He was walking towards the bushes near the car, apparently drawn by something lying on the ground. Ajay, coming closer, saw that it was an urn containing ashes, some of which seemed to have spilled out. Though the wrapping with the label was gone, it was the same kind of urn he'd picked up from the crematorium after his father's funeral. What a relief!

Ganesh had found his father's largely intact ashes, avoiding a horrendous loss.

"Look, sar," Ganesh said, smiling broadly. "We lost the puja items, but we can replace those easily. They didn't take the most important thing—which is irreplaceable. Now we can proceed."

Ajay unfolded his handkerchief and carefully wrapped the urn in it. Then they walked back to the row of stalls, where Ajay discovered that—luckily—he didn't have to recall what he'd lost. The puja items were conveniently available in a pre-packed bundle. They found the priest sitting next to his little tent, conducting the last rites in front of the man they'd seen earlier.

And then it was Ajay's turn. Removing his shirt and pants in the tent, he tied a dhoti around his waist and covered his shoulders with a plain towel. He crossed the riverbank, where there were more people now, and gingerly lowered himself in the moderately cold water. He shut his eyes and held his nose. The slight panic he felt at first dissipated after his head went in and out a few times, leaving his hair wet and plastered to the scalp.

He opened his eyes. Seeing marigold and jasmine petals scattered around him, trembling in the shimmery water, he thought of the phrase "earth to earth, ashes to ashes, dust to dust." It was from the Bible, he'd assumed, until he attended a funeral in the U.S., where a colleague told him the phrase was from the Book of Common Prayer. Ajay realized he didn't know a great deal about religion, any religion. Even what he knew about the Bhagavad Gita, which he'd only dipped into, mostly came from the stories of the epic Mahabharata, familiar to him since his childhood.

"How can you say you are agnostic without first learning about your own religion?" his father had once said, exasperated by Ajay's reluctance to accompany them to the temple.

"Calling it the religion I was *born into* is more accurate than saying *my* religion," Ajay had responded, incensing his father even more.

Looking back, perhaps an accurate description of Nana's reaction would be bewilderment. It was like the time when, as a boy, Ajay had been unwilling to learn swimming despite being coaxed by his father. After a couple of attempts, a fearful Ajay had refused to enter the water again, baffling his father. Would that be the word to sum up Nana's feelings? What's certain is that he turned out to be quite different from what his father had expected over the years.

"Om Namah Shivaya . . . Om Namah Shivaya . . . Om Namah . . . "

The deeply intoned chant drifted from the loudspeakers as Ajay slowly made his way back to the tent on the riverbank. It was warmer now, and his exposed upper body was almost dry by the time he sat in front of the priest, whose gnarled hands were arranging the items in preparation for the puja. Ajay bowed his head and repeated the priest's Sanskrit phrases, tripping over the words of an unfamiliar language. Another, more vivid memory came back to him. When he was leaving India, his parents accompanied him to the airport, where Nana embraced him unexpectedly at the last moment, his eyes filling with tears. It was the only time Ajay, who had been away at school when Kavita left for the U.S., saw his father cry.

The rites over and the ashes immersed, Ajay put on his dry clothes in the tent. Emerging, he paid the priest and joined Ganesh, who was patiently waiting for him. Wanting to call home before he left the site, Ajay took out his cellphone, which he'd switched off in the car to conserve battery power.

There were six missed calls. Ajay stared at the screen for a minute, and then dialed the home number.

Kavita picked up on the first ring. "Where are you?" she said.

"By the river, Akka. Just got done with immersing Nana's ashes. It went smoothly."

"What are you talking about? We've been trying to reach you."

"Yes, I saw that. Sorry. My phone was switched off. Is everything all right?"

"Ajay, I don't understand when you say that you immersed Nana's ashes. His ashes are still here. Amma is upset. I've been trying to call you."

"What do you mean, Akka? What ashes are you talking about?"

"You left the bag here. The urn was in it. We still have the ashes."

The previous night, when Ajay was having dinner at his mother's flat, the watchman who lived downstairs came to the door with the urn and said that Ganesh had arrived in the car to pick him up. The ashes couldn't be in the flat, per custom, so the watchman had kept the urn for Ajay. Now he was returning it. Ajay's mother, giving the watchman a bag containing the puja items, asked him to put the urn in it and give the bag to the driver. But when the watchman went down to the front gate, Ganesh wasn't there. He'd locked the car doors and gone to get a pack of cigarettes from the corner store.

Moments later, when the watchman got a call from another resident in the building, he put the bag down by the car, thinking that both Ajay and the driver would see it. They didn't. And it was only much later that the watchman, who was locking the gate, realized the bag had been left behind.

"That's terrible," Ajay mumbled, aghast. "I'm so sorry . . . I can't believe I left it behind."

Assuming the bag was already in the trunk, Ajay hadn't bothered to check. Like Ganesh, he'd been eager to hit the road for the long journey. So, whose urn had they picked up near the bushes? Some poor soul must have searched frantically for his loved one's ashes, wondering—just as Ajay had—how he'd perform the last rites.

Ajay saw himself picking up his father's real ashes and returning in a day or two, only to see the same priest again by the river. What would his reaction be? Shock, disbelief, horror? Ajay wanted to tell his sister that he'd gladly make another trip to the site.

But Kavita spoke first. "Ajay, I was talking to Amma earlier. Instead of rushing, she says, the rites should be performed in Banaras and the ashes immersed in the Ganges. I'm staying in India longer, so I can take care of it. I know you have to get back to the U.S. What do you think?"

Ajay paused, but only for a moment. "Yes, of course, Akka. You should go to Banaras."

INTERVIEW WITH THE WORLD'S OLDEST MAN

"What are you reading?" my dad asks. Twice.

Actually, I've stopped reading—I'm tired, having returned home late the previous night—but my head is bent low over the newspaper on my lap, and Nana, from where he sits in his recliner, can't see that my eyes are closed. Shaking off my drowsiness, I look up.

"It's today's paper, Nana. Would you like me to read from it?" Until his health deteriorated, my dad had been an avid newspaper reader. For as long as I can remember, even when we traveled in India, he'd never fail to pick up a daily paper—and sometimes, if we happened to be in the countryside, he'd pay to have an English-language paper sent to him from miles away.

"Let's talk," he says. "It's pretty quiet here, you know."

"Of course." I feel a stab of guilt. "I wanted to come earlier, but there was an unexpected business trip. Sorry. Is this place working out for you, Nana?"

He doesn't answer. Does that mean "yes," as I hope, or even "not sure," rather than "no." Whatever he means by the silence, I'm glad to leave it at that for the moment. What choice do I have, anyway? I often think I should be a good Indian son and keep him home and do all the right things—but then the thought overwhelms me and I push it out of my head.

"Is there any Indian food you crave, Nana? I'm sure they won't mind if I bring it. I can check with them."

"Forget that." He waves dismissively and then points at the newspaper on my lap. "Anything interesting?"

I'm struck by how frail he's become in recent months, with sagging cheeks and sallow skin, and I notice that his weathered hand is trembling. With his unshaven face and wispy, uncombed white hair, and a crumply shirt that's too big for his shrunken body, he seems a little lost. His eyes are glassy and his mouth twitches. I wonder what I'd find in the doctor's latest report.

I'm about to speak when a mechanical roar stops me, drawing our attention to the window. A lawn mower appears close to the building. A man with an impassive expression, wearing sunglasses, is standing erect on the mower, and for a few moments we only see his upper body, moving left-right-left like a juiced-up robot, before he disappears from view and the sound fades.

"I was reading about the First World War—or rather, the centennial remembrances," I say, folding the paper. "The war ended a hundred years ago. Can you guess what this article reminds me of?"

He looks puzzled. "Did I have my lunch?"

"I think you did, Nana. I saw Cynthia removing your tray when I got here. Are you hungry?"

"No. Just checking. Sometimes I forget, you know. How's Gita?"

"Rita is fine. She said she'd visit you this weekend with the kids."

Recalling the night Rita and I quarreled, after my late return from a business trip, I wince inwardly. I was exhausted—and, of course, so was she. Tempers flared, voices rose. And though the bedroom door was closed, I doubt that it prevented our shouted words from escaping down the stairwell in a mad rush and enter, like a rude intruder, the room where Nana was sleeping.

"What do you want me to do? Should I quit my job? I know it's a burden for you—"

"I didn't say that. But it's too much . . . I can't handle it. The help I'm getting is not enough. We need to do something."

"We will . . . this is temporary . . . "

Just a day after that exchange, when I walked into Nana's room with his cup of coffee, he said he was ready to move.

"Move where, Nana?"

"Old people's home, nursing home, whatever you want to call it. Where else?"

My attempts to allay his fears and delay the inevitable didn't work—and before I left the room, I knew he wasn't going to budge from his decision. Within a few weeks, our house was no longer my dad's home.

"The paper," Nana says, pointing again, and for a moment I think he wants to look at it. But, no, he's asking me to go back to what I was saying about the article I'd read.

"Well, it talks about how the hundredth anniversary of Armistice Day is being commemorated. It brought back memories of my interview. Do you remember that?"

"Yes," Nana says, surprising me. And he smiles at me for the first time that day.

When I was growing up in India, Nana had once casually mentioned—as he was reading the paper, I recall—that one of the world's oldest men lived in our ancestral village.

Stunned, I asked, "Nana, how do you know he's the oldest man in the world?"

"I said one of the oldest, not the oldest. But who knows? Some people in the village insist that nobody else is older. When I was a boy, I heard that he'd gone to Europe as a British Indian Army sepoy and fought briefly in the First World War. What's astonishing is the claim that he was older than Nehru, India's first prime minister, though younger than Gandhi."

I felt my spine tingle when Nana said that Nehru was born in 1889 and Gandhi in 1869!

"Can we go to the man's house?" I said. "I want to interview him." My vacation had just started and we were going to visit our ancestral village the following week.

My mother, who had overheard the conversation, stepped out of the kitchen and said, "We'll see . . . don't get your hopes up. The man is old and not well. I don't know if he'll be able to speak."

But he did speak, briefly. After Nana made inquiries and got permission from the old man's family, he took me to see him at their house in the village. We set out one morning, to the sound of chirping birds, and walked along a gravel road that skirted green paddy fields shimmering in the sunlight. It was a balmy November day, with a lively sea breeze that kept us cool and made the coconut and palm trees on the way sway decorously. The road curved and went past thatched huts, where many farm workers lived, before ending near a banana grove—behind which was a modest house with a sloping red-tiled roof. We stopped there and Nana knocked on the door.

A middle-aged man greeted him respectfully and led us to a room where the old man, shriveled with age, lay on a narrow bed, staring vacantly at the ceiling. He was toothless and almost hairless, with his hollowed cheeks giving him a mournful look, and he moved his lips constantly, as if he was saying a prayer. Until I entered the house, I'd been thrilled and was looking forward to this encounter. Surely, I thought, the newspaper Nana read every day would be eager to publish my grandly titled "Interview with the World's Oldest Man."

Now, becoming nervous, I wasn't sure if I could pull it off. The bulky tape recorder in my hand looked absurd. I wished it was less conspicuous, allowing me to slip it into my pocket.

Memory can play cruel tricks—it is so selective. The picture in my mind of our walk that lovely morning remains crisp, but it becomes blurry when I try to recall what was said. Perhaps the mood shift, from excitement to anxiety and embarrassment, had something to do with it. Nana had supported me, even reminding me to ask questions, but I don't recall opening my mouth.

The old man had rheumy eyes—he was sick, not to mention deaf—and what I remember most was his blank stare. We didn't spend much time there. My mother hadn't been keen on this outing, but Nana had indulged me—as had the old man's middle-aged relative, probably because my dad's family enjoyed a high status in the village. Now I felt sheepish about my intrusion.

But though I have no recollection of a conversation with the old man, it turns out—thanks to the audio tape, which surfaced not long ago when I was going through Nana's things—that we did speak briefly. The recording is a little scratchy, but I was able to listen to it after I found an old cassette player in the basement.

Me: *"When were you born? Do you remember the date?"*

Old man: *"What? Who's this boy?"*

The relative speaks in a loud voice.

Old man: *"Oh, I don't know. Is that a camera?"*

Me: *"No, it's a tape recorder. What were you doing in 1947, the year India gained independence?"*

Old man: *"What? Is he taking a picture?"*

Me: *"No, this is NOT a camera."*

Old man: *"What?"*

More loud talking, even shouting.

Old man: *"Oh, I became a farmer after returning from the Europe War—"*

Me: *"You mean the First World War? How much older was Gandhi?"*

Old man: *"What? Who?"*

Indistinct sounds, followed by loud talking.

Old man: *"Don't know . . . never saw him . . . "*

The recording ends abruptly.

"Well, the other day, I found the audio tape of the interview," I say. "Nana, I didn't know that you saved it."

He chuckles. "It was worth preserving, I guess."

"By the way, when Anita comes with her mother this weekend, she wants to interview you. She said that she wanted to ask her granddad about his family history and childhood days in India."

"Good," Nana says. "She can bring her recorder, but tell her that I'm not the world's oldest man. Far from it."

My cellphone pings. Reaching for it, I see that there's a text from Rita.

"I'm sure you have things to do . . . you've been here long enough," he says. "You should go now."

"I will, Nana, I will." I put my phone away, but don't get up from the chair to leave—yet.

DO YOU REMEMBER?

"Yes?" he said, staring at Jai, who had arrived early that day and was now greeting him.

The ailing old man, quietly waiting for his tea, scrunched up his sallow face—and Jai couldn't tell if his father was confused, as he tried to remember him, or annoyed. He'd changed drastically, his shrunken body and sunken eyes making him look so frail that Jai knew this would be his last trip to the country to see him. Through the chinks of the still-drawn blinds, whose color had changed over time from white to pale yellow, Jai could see slivers of sunlight entering the stuffy, dingy room. On the TV, tacked to a wall that appeared to have coffee stains, an anchor was reading the local news—but the old man, half-reclining in a retrofitted bed, scarcely looked at the screen. The chatter was background noise, and the TV's wavering glow provided ambient light. In his discolored eyes, as he gazed at Jai, there was no sign of recognition.

"Father, it's Jai."

"Where's Ranga?" the old man said, his voice low and raspy. Reaching for the bell next to his bed, he added, "My son is not here. Ranga can guide you if you're the new worker."

Ranga, holding a cup of milky tea, entered the room quickly, looking embarrassed. "Give it some time," he said to Jai softly. "He'll recognize you, eventually."

Shaken, Jai walked out without saying anything, though he smiled at Ranga. It was true that Jai had been largely absent from his father's life for a long time. Nevertheless, the old man's reaction came as a shock; he seemed to have no clue who Jai was—and he wasn't pretending.

In the kitchen, when the phone rang, Jai was pouring fresh coffee into his cup. Picking it up in the living room, he was pleased to hear his daughter's voice. They chatted for a while, mostly about her new school, which she'd begun attending after Jai and his wife decided to live apart. The separation was meant to be temporary, but now that Sheila had found a job and moved, he wasn't so sure. As they talked—or rather, as he listened to his daughter's report on the teachers she liked, the friends she'd made, and what she disliked about the school, Jai kept thinking how he should make sure his daughter would never become a stranger to him.

Hanging up the phone, Jai said, "That was my daughter . . . she's fourteen." He'd been watching a light brown gecko—whose buggy eyes and swiveling head gave it an extraterrestrial look—crawl tentatively near the window, when Ranga, returning to the living room, chased it out with a broom. Weren't geckos nocturnal? Did they bring bad luck or good luck, Jai wondered? Not that it mattered. What mattered, as Ranga seemed to agree, was that they didn't belong in the house.

"Happy to hear that," Ranga said. "Seems like your girl doesn't speak our language."

"Well, her mother grew up speaking English. That's our common language, both at home and outside."

"Not like here. I wouldn't understand people if I leave our region." Smiling, Ranga added, "My son is from another state, but he speaks our language because I got him as a baby."

"You adopted him?"

"This happened almost thirty years ago . . . things were a little different then. We bought our baby. He's married now and has a child of his own. They live separately, not far from me."

Jai was stumped, not so much because the revelation surprised him but because he couldn't think of a good response. Although curious, he was reluctant to ask more questions. He tended to be secretive about his own past, after all, sharing only the blandest details and being coy even with people he'd known a long time. Yet, when others chose to speak intimately about their lives, he didn't mind listening. When Sheila, during an argument, noted that an invisible wall separated them even after fifteen years of marriage, he didn't disagree.

Ranga, without any prompting, went on to say that he wished his son had studied further instead of dropping out of school to become a factory worker, shortly after a girl in the village caught his eye. Wanting to marry her, the son knew her parents would agree to the match only if he had a job. But it was going to be different with the next generation, Ranga said, because he'd make sure his granddaughter didn't drop out of school. He hoped she'd become a professional, and was pleased that his son and daughter-in-law agreed with him.

In fact, that was why Ranga, a widower, had come to the city. A good education required money, for which he couldn't rely on his son. And the village lacked opportunities. A relative had told Jai's siblings about Ranga, who was willing to stay in the flat and take care of their bedridden father, also a widower. Following their mother's death not long ago, the siblings had taken turns to keep an eye on their father, often by moving in temporarily. Now it was Jai's turn—although he realized that after all these years, he was more of an outsider.

Later that morning, Jai thought his father was sleeping when he peeked in, but the old man opened his eyes as if he'd been expecting him. "Can you sweep the room . . . it's been a few days?" he said. "And I'm ready for my bath. Turn on the geyser for the hot water."

Once when Jai was playing with his daughter, she'd struck him on the face with unexpected force, dislodging his spectacles. They didn't break, luckily, but he recalled how—when his vision blurred momentarily—he'd been astonished that his little girl could be so strong. Now he felt a similar sense of bewilderment. Recovering quickly, Jai said he'd get to it right away.

Ranga was horrified when he saw him sweeping the floor, but when he tried to intervene, Jai told him not to worry. Taking him to the living room, Jai said the best thing to do now was to humor his father and pretend that he was an employee. "It's temporary," he said when Ranga expressed skepticism. "We'll take it one day at a time. Let's see what happens."

Jai embraced his new role with gusto. After sweeping the room and making sure the water was ready for his father's bath, he said, "Okay, I'll ask Ranga to give me a hand."

Over the next few days, Jai got to know Ranga. Stocky and barrel-chested, with a stubbly, lined and sunburned face that reflected years of toil in the farmland surrounding his village, Ranga usually wore baggy khaki shorts and a faded T-shirt. Though affable and chatty, he could, in an instant, become morose when he missed his village or got a call from his son, who seemed to be perennially short of money. Ranga would sometimes scold his son, or complain to Jai.

"He spends more than he earns," he once said. "Thinks I'm an ATM!"

Ranga could neither read nor write, but he had a sharp memory, allowing him to keep track of details. A health aide came to the flat every day to check on Jai's father and spend some time with him, giving Ranga a break. Knowing that life in the flat was constricting, Jai encouraged him to go out more often—but Ranga seldom ventured far, noting that the density and chaos of urban life scared him a little. He had no idea what an ATM was, he said, until his move to the city. Now Ranga had a proper account, and a lady at the bank helped him whenever he wanted to deposit or withdraw money.

His hair had turned white and he was missing a couple of teeth, but Ranga was so nimble and strong—he could lift Jai's father like a baby with his callused hands—that Jai realized he was younger than he looked. The old man relied on him so much that Jai's role in the flat was marginal for the most part. Even after almost a week, he treated Jai as little more than Ranga's assistant. While he said "Jai" now instead of "hey" when addressing him, the name didn't seem to evoke any memories. To his father, Jai remained a domestic worker.

Another surprise awaited Jai.

"Madam is coming today," Ranga announced when, on the first Sunday after his arrival, Jai was flipping through the newspaper over a cup of coffee. "She comes every week."

"Who comes every week?"

"Shaila Madam. She comes to see your father."

A stunned Jai sank back in his chair. He hadn't expected to hear that name, a name which stirred long-buried emotions. He'd lost contact with her years ago, while they were still in college, and it came as a jolt that she was in touch with the family.

Jai had first met his wife at a party, and he recalled how—because of the chatter around them—he'd misheard the name when she was introduced to him. For a confusing moment, Sheila had sounded like Shaila. Did that play a role, albeit subconsciously, in the immediate attraction he'd felt for Sheila?

Jai wanted to ask when Shaila started coming to the house, but a loud ring stopped him. His father was calling.

"I'll go," Jai said, rising quickly. "You can finish your breakfast."

"I need my shirt," the old man said when Jai entered the room. "Shaila is coming."

"Sure, let me get it." Moving towards the dresser, Jai saw the thick folder he'd been trying to avoid. It contained the medical records that were bound to tell him all about his father's condition—although frankly, he was afraid to find out more. Jai had become, even before the old man's decline, a stranger.

"Oddly detached" were the words Jai's wife once used to describe him. "Sometimes, it seems to me, you're an observer more than a participant," she'd said to Jai during an argument. "I feel that you're somewhere else even when we're together, when we're in the same room."

Unlike his siblings, who were much older, Jai did not grow up in one place. Had his itinerant childhood—limiting the opportunity to form lasting attachments—made him more different that he otherwise would have been? And, surely, his migration to another country had played a big role. Whatever the reasons, he'd never felt like an insider anywhere. The word "foreign" didn't feel foreign; it felt familiar.

When Shaila arrived, Jai wondered, as he was greeting her, if he'd have recognized her on the street. Yes, but it would have taken him a minute, a second glance—because Jai had last seen her over two decades ago. She had changed, as did he. "Smart, charismatic, bohemian, alluring" was how he'd have described her in college, where her youthful idealism and intensity had drawn him. And he wasn't the only one smitten by her. Now, he thought, she could easily pass for a respectable, middle-aged college lecturer. Actually, as he soon found out, she was a school principal.

Shaila had preferred a no-nonsense approach, and it wasn't different now. Her grey-flecked hair was tied in a loose knot, her casual attire included a lime green tunic top, and her canvass shoes—which she left outside before entering the room—were well suited for walking. When she took off her spectacles and plopped on the sofa, after handing Ranga a bag of oranges and bananas, Jai was suddenly transported back to his college days. Surely, it was because of her eyes—big, dark, searching—which he remembered so well. They'd held him from the moment of their first meeting on campus, where she was handing out fliers to students and asking them to join a protest gathering.

"I'm sorry . . . I cannot come," he'd mumbled, although he took a flier. "I've to finish my work. My assignment is due soon."

Shaila, without speaking, let him pass—but he was stung by the mockery in her smiling eyes, and his face turned red. Despite that unpromising start, they got to know each other well. It turned out that she already knew about him because their fathers had been classmates in school. The parents were pleased when Jai and Shaila became friends, even though they didn't know that there was more to it. But there were also boundaries—not unusual back then for couples who weren't married. Jai and Shaila had jokingly referred to the relationship that wasn't just a friendship as their "freelationship."

Entering the old man's room with Shaila, Jai saw his face light up with a smile.

"How are you, daughter?" he said, extending his hand from the armchair. Freshly shaven and bathed, with his hair neatly combed, he looked dapper in his clean white kurta and loose-fitting pants. He hadn't called him "son" in a long time, Jai thought, marveling at his transformation in Shaila's presence. Relaxed, even cheerful, the old man asked her to sit next to him.

And then, looking at Jai, he said with unexpected sharpness, "Don't just stand there . . . get some water and make tea for the guest!"

Jai saw the shocked expression on Shaila's face, but he hurried away before she could protest.

"The work ethic is not the same these days," he could hear his father saying. "In the old days, you didn't have to tell them everything. They knew what to do when there was a visitor."

Shaila didn't say anything to Jai when he brought the tea and snacks, but she glanced at him quizzically several times. Jai merely smiled. Remaining silent, he was an unobtrusive server, hovering near the door in case his father needed anything, and returning only to take the cups and plates. Thankfully, the visit ended without further awkwardness.

When Shaila exited the flat after saying goodbye, Jai followed her.

"How extraordinary!" she said as soon as they got to the stairs. "What was that all about, Jai? I could hardly believe it, and I desperately wanted to say something. Your father doesn't know who you are?"

Jai's smile felt more like a grimace. "It's complicated. Let's get out of the building first."

It was oppressive outside, and the sunlight bright despite predictions of rain, as Jai felt the heat rise from the earth to envelope him in a humid bubble. Instinctively, they moved towards the shade of a quietly swaying banyan tree that had miraculously survived the onslaught of construction in the area. The sturdy gnarled vines gave it the appearance of a modern sculpture, although Jai knew the tree belonged to an earlier period—a more gracious time in the city—when such verdant foliage had been plentiful, lining streets that were quieter and less congested. As he looked up at this solitary tree, its branches seemed to shake mournfully.

"Wow, it's no time to be outside," he said, feeling icky. His undershirt, already damp, began sticking to the skin. "We should have called a cab to take you home. Actually, if you don't mind me saying, I thought a school principal would come in a car."

She smiled, and for a moment Jai thought he saw that old mockery in her eyes.

"Our school is far from fancy, Jai. As for the weather, I'm used to it. I think you've been away so long that you forgot how it's here at this time. Let's talk more over a cold drink . . . we've to catch up. But first, what on earth is going on between you and your father? I'm baffled!"

"So was I, Shaila. Nothing is happening between us—that's the problem! He doesn't know who I am. I'm just playing along for now. His memory is gone, of course, and he thinks I'm a domestic worker. To be honest, I'm fine with that for now. I won't be here for long."

An autorickshaw was parked under the tree, and its dozing driver had just woken up. They got in for the short ride to Cloves & Cardamom, which was almost empty in the lethargic post-lunch period, giving them both peace and privacy in the cool, partially dark interior. Jai, at first reflexively avoiding any discussion about *his* past, spoke after they ordered their drinks.

"Did you know that Ranga bought his son, almost three decades ago?" he said.

"Yes, I know that," she said, looking irritated. Pausing, she added, "You act like a foreigner, Jai, as if you didn't know. Don't you remember what we were agitating against in college?"

"Indeed, I do. Child labor. The building contractor hired by the college was using child labor for his projects, and we—"

"Yes, yes, but that wasn't the only thing. Remember how, even after the administration investigated and rescinded the contract, we continued our agitation because of what was going on? Children were being bought and sold, not only because somebody wanted to adopt one."

Of course he did. That's when the agitation spun out of control, leading to the cancelation of classes and the postponement of exams. Moreover, the turmoil on campus didn't bring about further changes. The city's ban on child labor came later, only after a new government came to power. Primary education became mandatory then, but it was also true that the use of child labor continued in pockets of the city, often secretly.

During that turbulent year in college, as the student activists became more radical, Jai was filled with uneasiness. Elated by their early success, they'd become too bold, even arrogant, in his opinion. Initially skeptical, Jai had joined the agitators because of Shaila—but then, while he'd been just as happily surprised by their victory, he was reluctant to go any further. The passions it unleashed seemed alarming, not admirable. Besides, being single-mindedly ambitious, Jai knew he would have to work hard and do well to get the financial aid he needed to study abroad. If the activists saw him as an escapee rather than a stayer who tried to solve problems, so be it.

When Jai had told her, before the year ended, that he was transferring to another college, hundreds of miles away, she was taken aback.

"Why now?" she'd asked, her face showing disappointment. Activism had made her life meaningful and she was delighted that they'd become good comrades, she added. The word "comrades" made him squirm. But she wasn't joking. Why was he walking away now, she said, turning his back on a cause that was worth fighting for, especially after they'd tasted the sweetness of success? She spoke calmly, and Jai was struck by the force of her convictions.

I don't agree with the increasingly strident ways of the activists, and the disruption they cause, he'd wanted to say. But he didn't. Instead, Jai said he wanted to focus on his studies—which was also true, though he knew it sounded like a cop out, an admission of failure.

Shaila said she understood, smiling sadly. And Jai realized, even before he could tell her which college he was heading to, that things would never be the same again between them.

"Prosopamnesia."

"Excuse me?" Jai said, looking up with a puzzled expression. Having paid the waiter, he was putting his wallet away.

"Sorry, the word just popped out." Shaila laughed softly. "Jai, I was thinking about your father. It could be prosopamnesia. Recognizing new faces is difficult—"

"I'm hardly a new face, Shaila!"

"Of course. What I mean is that you haven't been here in a while. I'm not an expert, obviously, but when a patient has prosopamnesia, I believe the neurological damage tends to be selective. Anyway, that's my take on what happened. I haven't spoken to your sister, and I was reluctant to look at the medical report in front of your dad. It was on the dresser. Have you read it?"

"No, I haven't, but I will read it soon." Jai didn't say that he'd been avoiding it. And his recent conversations with family members, he was reluctant to mention, had been perfunctory. Unsurprisingly, he didn't know much about his father's condition.

"In my case, he sees me regularly," Shaila said, picking up her spectacles as she stood up. "Stick around, Jai. He'll get used to you. My hope is that he'll recognize you if you give it enough time."

Jai smiled. "Yes, Shaila, that's also my hope . . . and that's what Ranga said as well. Let's see."

When they stepped out of Cloves & Cardamom, the contrast—in terms of light, temperature, sound—was so striking that he stood still without talking for a few moments, blinking rapidly. His sunglasses, which he'd forgotten to bring from the flat, would have been nice. Shading his eyes, he stepped over to the bus shelter near the restaurant. Before they parted, he wanted to ask her something. Jai had hesitated because it was an awkward question, but it was now or never. Had she been expelled from the college?

"No," she responded. After all the chaos on campus, she'd just decided to drop out.

Ah, the chaos. Jai had heard about it, in bits and pieces. He'd stayed in touch with her initially, but that ended when he found out that she and the group leader had become close—"an item," as a former classmate put it. Soon, Jai ceased to keep up with the news from his old college.

It was only later, while on a visit home, that he heard more about the turmoil. A few activists, including that student leader, had gone on a fast after issuing their demands. It triggered unrest on campus and, after a period of uncertainty, the local government responded harshly, deploying the police and arresting the activists. Some students were expelled, though Jai got conflicting reports about Shaila. He could have checked with her family or her friends and tried to track her down—but he didn't. And then, his break over, he went back to his college.

The bus shelter looked new and surprisingly comfortable. It was an example, albeit a small one, of the improvements that locals liked to talk about, sometimes accusing Jai of being willfully blind to the good changes taking place in the city, while focusing on the negatives.

"You're stuck in the past, my friend," one of them said in exasperation. "You should visit more often, and stop making subconscious comparisons between *here* and *there*. Then you'll learn."

The man had a point, so Jai didn't argue with him. But he could also sense a certain defensiveness in that posture, an assertion of local pride, and perhaps an unwillingness to be judged by a non-local. Random comments from a person who had cut his ties often held little value for the locals.

Jai wished he and Shaila could have chatted more in the restaurant, but he knew she had to leave. In the shelter, though, Shaila didn't seem to be in a rush, and she continued to talk.

"I knew you had left the country, and I knew what you were up to . . . kind of," she said. "But I hesitated to get in touch . . . after so many years. I decided to wait for your visit."

"I wish I'd known, Shaila. But what happened . . . after you left the college, I mean?"

"It was a rough time . . . a surreal time. You heard about the arrests and expulsions, right? Well, there was also a death . . . in police custody. They claimed it was a heart attack, triggered by shock and hunger. We didn't believe them. A lot of people didn't know because it was hushed up."

Jai was speechless. He saw her eyes cloud, and the sadness he detected touched him. Though he didn't ask, he was sure that it was the group leader who had died. Would it be appropriate to give her a hug, he wondered, even if he didn't say anything? Probably not.

"It all happened so long ago, Jai," she said, recovering. "It was a different era."

Following the crackdown, a disenchanted Shaila left the college and drifted aimlessly for a few years, even becoming estranged from her family. Then, thanks to the support of a few friends, she got involved in social work and attended another college to finish her degree. While training to be a teacher, she met the man who would become her husband and the father of her two children. Reconciling with her father took a while—but it did happen, and after her mother died some years ago, they became close again. The previous year, before her father's death, he'd asked her to contact his old friend—Jai's father—and visit him once in a while.

"My visits became a little more regular after your father's health declined," she said. "But Jai, we can talk later. I can see the bus from here. That's the one I need to take."

"A bus!" Jai said, appalled. "I thought we were just standing here to talk. Please take a cab."

She laughed, as if he'd cracked a joke. "I'm used to it," she said. "I don't have to go far. But here's an auto . . . I'll take an auto."

The passing autorickshaw had slowed to a crawl, with the driver looking at them expectantly, when Shaila flagged him down. He swerved and pulled over.

Heartened by Shaila's laugh, which ended the gloomy mood, Jai held up the business card she'd given him earlier. "I like the name of your school, by the way," he said. "Wish I'd gone to a school called Fun Academy. I might have had a more pleasant experience as a student."

"It was called Foundational Academy when we took over," she said, smiling. "That name was a little boring and long, so we changed it to Fun Academy."

"Very appropriate."

Getting into the autorickshaw, Shaila settled back and gave the driver her address. Then, turning to Jai, she said: "I told Ranga to send his granddaughter to our school. It will be good for her. He was very excited. He's going to talk to his son and let me know."

Revving up, the autorickshaw pulled away with a roar—and as Jai waved, he was greeted by a billow of exhaust mixed with shimmering dust.

ON DISTANT SHORES

WHERE THE GRASS IS GREENER

"Fifteen years," Shashi boomed into the phone. "I can't believe it's been that long since we last spoke!"

Ram was in his office that afternoon, about to break for lunch, when he got the call from Shashi, who said he had tracked him down by—what else?—searching on the internet. "I'm in town for a conference," Shashi added. "I came from India last week. I'm hoping we can meet today."

"Absolutely," Ram said, trying to absorb the shock of hearing from his former friend after all these years. Feeling tongue-tied, he stood with the phone near the window and looked out, letting Shashi do most of the talking. A thundershower that morning had washed all the cars in the parking lot, where they now stood gleaming in the sunlight, quietly waiting for their owners to reclaim them later in the day. Finally finding his voice, Ram offered to meet Shashi at the hotel.

"I'd also like to meet your wife, Ram, unless you think it's not a good idea."

"An excellent idea, Shashi," he said, flustered. "Nalini would love to meet you. I'll pick you up."

That wasn't necessary, Shashi said. A local attendee and fellow environmentalist lived in Ram's subdivision, and he'd offered to drop Shashi at Ram's house after their conference.

After hanging up, Ram called Nalini to inform her. Then, leaving his office early, he got into his car and drove home with trepidation in the afternoon traffic. Considering how his friendship with Shashi had ended, he was more than a little nervous about this unexpected and unwelcome reunion.

"You seem tense," Nalini said. "I thought you had a good chat with him."

"Yes, I did." Ram stopped flipping the TV channels and put the remote control down. "But, you know, it's been fifteen years . . . things change. I never expected to hear from Shashi, let alone see him again."

"Why not? I thought you had been friends in India."

The doorbell rang, cutting off their conversation, and Ram almost tripped as he hurried to the foyer and opened the door. Breaking into a wide smile, Shashi greeted him effusively and, to Ram's surprise, even spread out his arms for an embrace. He'd put on weight and his thinning hair was almost completely grey, making him look older than his age—but for Ram, that engaging sprightliness was instantly recognizable, bringing back memories of their close friendship. The car, having already backed out of the driveway, was on its way to the street behind Ram's house.

"It's good to see you, Shashi, after such a long time," Ram said, ushering him into the living room, where Nalini was waiting. The conversation flowed without any awkwardness, although they stuck to banal pleasantries. That changed after a round of drinks.

"So how did you and Ram meet?" Shashi asked, smiling.

If Nalini was surprised by the question, she didn't show it. Laughing, she sipped her wine and brushed back her wavy, jet-black hair with a flick of the wrist. She'd changed into a canary yellow salwaar-kameez. "You should ask your friend here," she said. "I'm surprised he hasn't told you yet."

"Well, you know how it's been," Ram said. "We didn't stay in touch." Aware that Nalini and Shashi were gazing at him, Ram suddenly became preoccupied with his drink, as if he'd seen something unsavory in his glass. There was a serious, almost stricken expression on his face and he didn't look up.

"I was wondering about that," Nalini said. "Did you—?"

"We just drifted apart, more or less," Ram cut in. "The fact that I was here and Shashi was in India made it a little complicated." Even as he spoke, without looking at Nalini or Shashi, Ram wondered how convincing he sounded.

"That's interesting," Shashi said, following a pause. "I thought there was more to it, but I can see what you mean."

The phone rang. It was a business call for Nalini, who took the cordless from Ram and, excusing herself, left the room.

"I didn't tell Nalini about Priya," Ram said gently.

"I thought as much, Ram." Shashi looked through the large bay window at the newly built deck in the backyard, where, even in the fading golden light, one could see the dogwood trees and flowering shrubs—including azaleas, honeysuckles and lilacs—that had bloomed in vibrant colors.

"Do you remember how we used to joke about students who were obsessed with America?" Shashi continued. "What was it we used to say?"

"Where is the grass greener?"

"And the answer would be, 'Where the land is paved with greenbacks and green cards.' Yes, I remember now!"

They laughed at this old one-liner, although Ram felt a spasm of discomfort at the same time. "Shashi, you knew I couldn't come to India because of my visa situation. And you know how long it takes even after getting—"

"I know. We were just surprised that it meant so much to you. But don't get me wrong. I think Nalini is wonderful."

"Yes, she is. I'm fortunate. I deeply regret, though, that Priya and I had to end our relationship the way we did. How is she these days?"

"Fine, Ram. Her husband joined a new company, so they'll be shifting soon. They have a daughter."

"Are we ready to leave?" Nalini asked, a quizzical smile on her face.

Startled by her sudden appearance, Ram mumbled, "Yes, of course." He wondered if she'd heard the last bit of their conversation.

Earlier, they'd decided to have dinner at an Indian-Chinese restaurant. There wasn't much chatting on the way and even Nalini seemed a little subdued in the car. Ram and Shashi had met as college students in India, hitting it off on the very first day. Looking back, Ram found it hard to say what it was that had initially attracted them to each other. Ram, just out from a boarding school, felt like a duck out of water in the new environment, where most students had attended schools in that state and, unlike Ram, spoke the local language fluently. Shashi was one such student and, in fact, English had been his second language in school. But he was a quick learner, Ram realized, with a keen interest in his studies.

Sometimes, in the classes they took together, Ram sought help from Shashi, who was always genial and approachable. They became close friends and remained roommates until graduation, following which Ram stayed with Shashi's family while looking for a job. And then, just a few months after joining an IT company, Ram got a work visa for the U.S. The decision to go abroad was momentous, changing his life in many ways. America had never been on their radar in college; on the contrary, they'd sometimes made fun of students who seemed excessively fixated on America and college admission tests like GRE, GMAT and TOEFL.

Ram, however, got swept up in the excitement of that period's tech boom, and the two friends found they no longer agreed on where their futures lay. It shouldn't have affected things, given their strong ties, except that Ram's decision to go abroad had other consequences.

At the restaurant, they ordered a bottle of Riesling and before long the words began to tumble again, although Ram and Shashi avoided any mention of their past. But Nalini, who had uncharacteristically drunk more than one glass of wine, went back to the question she'd been asking in the house. The food having arrived by now, they helped themselves to crunchy Chicken 65 and steaming, pungently fragrant dishes of Chili prawns, Gobi Manchurian and Haka noodles.

"Fifteen years—that's a long time," Nalini said, smiling. "So what happened? Or am I being too nosy?"

"No, you're not," Shashi said. "We drifted apart. Maybe the distance proved to be a barrier, as Ram implied."

"Not really." Ram's voice was so low they could barely hear him. "I was once engaged to Shashi's sister, Priya."

Nalini and Shashi stopped eating and stared at Ram, who had become quite still. He could hear his heart thumping as his eyes stayed focused on the plate in front of him. For a few moments, though it seemed longer, all they heard was the sound of silverware and murmuring voices from the other tables.

"That was a while ago," Shashi said, ending the tense pause. "Why bring it up now?"

Nalini's face had turned pale, and she hastily drank some water, as if to clear an obstruction in her throat. "How come you never told me this?" she said, her voice trembling.

Ram, not looking up, remained silent.

"Please, let's not talk about this," Shashi said, looking distressed. "I didn't mean to cause any trouble."

Rising abruptly, Nalini picked up her purse and said she'd wait for them outside the restaurant. After Ram paid the bill, they all piled into the car and remained mostly silent on the way to Shashi's hotel. Shashi had politely declined to spend the night with them, noting that he'd be waking up early to catch the airport shuttle.

As soon as Ram tuned off the ignition, on reaching their house, Nalini got out wordlessly and went up to the bedroom. Feeling jittery, Ram lingered in the family room and turned on the television, but he didn't watch anything. Nalini was sleeping, with the light on her side turned off, when he eventually entered the bedroom. Tossing and turning, he spent a restless night, only to fall into a deep slumber just before dawn. In his dream, he saw Priya on a domestic flight while visiting India. As Ram flipped through an airline magazine, and Nalini beside him looked out the window, he happened to see Priya passing by in the aisle. She noticed him at the same time, the shocked expression on her face quickly changing to a smile. There was only time for casual hellos, since the passengers behind Priya were trying to reach their seats.

"Who is she?" Nalini asked.

"Somebody I knew when I used to live here," Ram said softly.

But Priya, who was still close by, heard him. "It was more than that," she said, turning around. "Ram and I were engaged to be married."

The chatter in the vicinity stopped, and Ram realized that a few passengers were glaring at him.

Although Nalini looked stunned, she managed to speak. "How come you never told me? Did you break off your engagement to her before you met me?"

When Ram didn't respond, he saw that Nalini's eyes were moist.

Shards of sunlight entered through the window and caressed Ram's face, ending his dream. He'd overslept. Nalini had already gone to work, and when the smell of coffee didn't greet him in the kitchen, he realized that she'd left without brewing the usual pot for the two of them. Deciding to work from home, Ram turned on the coffee machine and carried his laptop to the dining table. With the uninterrupted stillness of the house keeping him company, Ram remained absorbed in his project for the next several hours. Throughout the day, thoughts of Nalini lurked at the back of his mind.

It was in an elevator, while on his way to a job interview, that Ram first saw Nalini. She, too, had come for an interview at that firm. A moment of awkwardness followed, but Ram was relieved when he found out they were not competing for the same position. They talked briefly and, after exchanging business cards, wished each other good luck.

Ram didn't get the job, and he wondered how Nalini had fared. She phoned him first to ask how the search was going but seemed reluctant to talk about herself—at least, initially. Then finally, speaking in an apologetic tone, she told him the firm had offered her a job. It was the position Ram had applied for. He was momentarily out of breath, as if somebody had slapped him. But recovering quickly, Ram offered his congratulations.

"No, no," she said. "I'm not taking it. That's not the job I applied for. I don't know why they—"

"Because they were impressed by you, Nalini, and felt you'd be good for the position. Listen, please don't make a hasty decision. Why don't we meet for a cup of coffee and talk it over."

He'd spoken impulsively and didn't know what there was to discuss. It was her decision, after all, and Ram knew he was being presumptuous even as he spoke. Surprisingly, however, she agreed to meet him. The following day, in a café, Nalini's unaffected charm and amiable manner put him at ease.

"I hope you take the job," Ram said, putting down the steaming cups of coffee. "It's a good opportunity."

Nalini smiled but didn't say anything. Suddenly it dawned on Ram that she'd already turned down the offer. Her reason for agreeing to see him was different. His heart gave a lurch, although the thrill he experienced was mingled with anxiety. He'd been unhappy for a few months now, not only because he was struggling to find a suitable job but also because he didn't know how to end his engagement to Priya. He hadn't seen her in two years and felt their relationship had reached a dead end. But Priya and her family didn't seem to think so. It was his closeness to the family, and a fondness for Priya, that had led to the unofficial engagement. Given their traditional background, there had been no courtship in the conventional sense.

Ram and Nalini started dating, but he lost his nerve when it came to telling her about Priya. A bigger blunder was that he didn't call Priya immediately and explain everything. His lack of judgment had led to deception, Ram realized sorrowfully, and he'd ended up hurting both women.

Closing his laptop, Ram reached for the yellow legal pad near him. Then, in a carefully worded letter that avoided being defensive, he told Nalini what had happened. After struggling to end it on the right note, Ram decided that anything other than a brief explanation would be inadequate, even inappropriate, on paper. Whatever else he had to express—words filled with feeling, gestures laced with meaning—could only be done in person. Ram folded the sheet of paper and left it on the kitchen counter. Stretching to relax his tense body, he realized that Nalini would be home in an hour. He took out his recipe book, which he had meticulously compiled but seldom used, and began to cook. As the light outside began to dim, a pleasing aroma filled the kitchen, and when Ram finally turned off the stove, it was with a sense of satisfaction that he decided to go for a walk.

Although it wasn't raining, Ram took an umbrella with him. Otherwise, if a thunderstorm arrived like an unannounced guest, as it often did these days, there would be no time to find refuge. An afternoon shower had left the air crisp, and now as the daylight completely seeped out of the sky, turning dusk to darkness, Ram felt invigorated by the brisk walk. Returning to the house, he saw that Nalini's car was back in the port.

The motion-sensor lights sprang to life, casting a bright glow on the driveway and a big chunk of the lawn. The grass had grown fast because of the rain and in places it had coiled into glistening tufts of greenery. He would have to mow the lawn soon. As Ram approached the side door, he noticed that the kitchen blinds were still open. Nalini, who was taking out dinner plates from the cabinet, turned to look out. Ram saw her face only for a moment, but he was certain she'd smiled at him. He hurried forward and opened the door.

INDIAN UNCLE SAM

Standing near the revolving baggage carousel, as he nervously waited for his mother and sister, Prakash unfolded the note and read it again. *Got to have the rent by Tuesday. If you cannot pay, you'll have to vacate the apartment. Sorry.* He'd found it that morning, wedged in the crack of his front door, just as he was leaving for the airport. Brad must have left it there last night. The terse ultimatum stung, considering that Brad, the manager of Sunrise Apartments, had seemed to understand Prakash's dilemma when they'd talked the previous week about his outstanding rent.

"I need another month to sort things out, Brad," he'd said. "Diwali is coming up."

"What's that?"

"A festival of lights that's big in India. My mother and sister are visiting from there. I can't ask them to cancel their trip . . . would be very awkward. We're going to celebrate Diwali. They bought their tickets weeks ago."

"I understand, Praycash. Good wishes to you on this happy occasion. Unfortunately I have no control; I only work in this place. But I'll speak to the boss and let you know."

The place, Prakash couldn't help thinking, was beginning to look bedraggled. The property used to be well maintained, but that changed after the staff cuts—and now, sitting in Brad's office, he could see the uncut lawn and unpicked trash in the parking lot, where there weren't as many cars these days. Sad. In the wake of the economic downturn, more apartments had fallen vacant in recent months, casting a pall on Sunrise Apartments, which had been Prakash's home for over two years.

At the airport, Prakash was putting the note back in his pocket when he spotted his mother and . . . wait a minute! The other woman *wasn't* Sujata, his sister; she looked like Chitra. It *was* Chitra. Stunned, Prakash waited as they looked around uncertainly, but when they saw him, he quickly stepped forward to greet them. His mother appeared tired, even disoriented, after the long flight—and Chitra, smiling tentatively, was perhaps wondering how he'd react to her unannounced arrival.

"What a pleasant surprise," Prakash said, reaching for Chitra's carry-on suitcase.

"Are you sure?" She laughed. For a moment he couldn't figure out what Chitra was referring to: his greeting or his offer to help.

Prakash soon found out that the firm his sister worked at had been bought out, leaving all the employees unsure of their jobs. Sujata realized she couldn't afford to leave India just then, but for reasons that remained unclear to him, he hadn't been informed of the plan to ask Chitra to accompany their mother on her trip. Was this a clumsy attempt to set them up—again? Prakash had known Chitra, his sister's former classmate, while they were still in college—but they hadn't talked much until his last visit to India about a year ago, when his mother, after mentioning that Chitra was single and lived not far from her house, hinted that she'd make a good match for him. He deftly steered the conversation away from the topic. When she brought it up again, saying, "Prakash, why don't you just meet her for dinner; I'm sure you'll have a lot to talk about," he surprised himself by responding, "Sure, I'll be glad to if she's interested."

Their outing—Prakash hesitated to call it a date—started a little awkwardly, but it went well as the evening progressed and they ended up having a pleasant conversation over a delicious meal. As he saw it, they both knew that a relationship would not work when they were living so far apart. And there was no question of making a decision, as his mother had probably hoped, after just a couple of meetings. Getting to know each other was important. But that wasn't logistically possible unless he moved back to India. Prakash left it at that, calling Chitra only to say goodbye before he flew back to the U.S.

After paying the parking fee, Prakash joined the caravan of vehicles leaving the airport, driving slowly until they got on the highway. Glancing in the mirror, he noticed that his mother—sitting in the back, at her insistence—had already dozed off. Surreptitiously, he looked again at Chitra, who was sitting beside him as she gazed at the passing vehicles. Prakash wanted to explain why he hadn't been in touch with her lately. But the timing seemed inappropriate. In any case, his mother woke up soon and started talking. As she gave him an update on things back home, Prakash listened, speaking only occasionally to answer a question. It didn't take long to reach Sunrise Apartments.

It was the start of a long weekend, thankfully. So for the next three days Prakash didn't have to explain why he wasn't going to work. His mother and Chitra had many questions, as they gradually adjusted to the changes—and whenever they marveled at the novelty of America, Prakash was reminded of his own early days in the country. The two women took over his household, despite his protests, making him feel as if he was back in India. Despite the Tuesday deadline, Prakash was grateful for the female, not to mention filial, companionship that had been missing from his life.

The impending eviction, if he couldn't come up with the full amount he owed, seemed unreal at this point. Yet it could happen, just like that. Although his last job interview had actually gone very well, the competition was stiff and he didn't get picked, to his intense disappointment. Prakash had tucked away some money for expenses, but touching it to pay the rent would be risky. Somehow, he'd have to defer it—at least until his mother and Chitra went back to India. He couldn't afford to be broke now.

Rising early on Tuesday, Prakash got ready quietly, as if he were going to work as usual. He thought his mother and Chitra were still sleeping, but the light was on in the kitchen, where the smell of brewing coffee greeted him and he saw Chitra seated at the table, flipping through a magazine.

"Going to the office early?" she said, smiling. "The coffee is almost ready. I can fix you some breakfast."

"No, that's fine." He was uneasy. "You're up early, Chitra. Hope you slept okay."

"Yes . . . I'm an early riser. But, Prakash, I did want to say something before you left. When I agreed to accompany your mother, I should have insisted on informing you. Making it a surprise visit wasn't a good idea. We didn't plan it well. I can see that it came as a rude shock. You may think we have nefarious motives." She smiled again.

"No, no, that's nonsense, Chitra. Believe me, I'm absolutely delighted to see you. If I seem preoccupied, it's because of a work issue. But it'll be fine. Let's have a nice long chat this evening. We can go out for dinner."

Prakash didn't linger. Swallowing his coffee, he picked up his brief bag and, saying goodbye, hurried out. Brad was not in yet at the rental office. Getting into his car, Prakash drove in the direction of his former office. A mild panic gripped him. How did it come to this—so quickly?

Not long ago, he had a nice job with no worries and was living comfortably, looking forward to the day when he'd be able to make a down payment on a spacious condo in a lively, attractive neighborhood. And now, unbelievably, he was close to being homeless. When the economy tanked and Prakash got laid off, he had thought—like many others—the setback would be temporary. But even after turning his job hunt into a full-time effort, there was no success, although he did get called for interviews. Those interviews, he now realized, had given him false hope. The money he'd saved was dwindling rapidly. Given his visa status, unless he found another job soon, his time in America would come to an end, dashing or putting a hold on his dreams.

Prakash reached the building where he used to work, only to feel silly and self-conscious. It was a pointless drive. Not wanting to be seen by his former colleagues, he abruptly turned around and drove back to Sunrise Apartments and parked in front of the rental office—which was, fortunately, not visible from his apartment. Seeing Brad's car, Prakash felt a surge of hope—and dread. Opening the door, he greeted Brad, who was looking through some papers at his cluttered desk. A shriveled bouquet drooped from a vase next to the computer. Like many things here, these flowers needed attention.

There was a discomfiting pause.

"Good morning," Brad said. "Ah . . . do you have the check, Praycash?"

"No, I don't, Brad. Can you give me one more extension? I'll borrow the money, if needed, and pay you in full next month. My mother is here, as I said, along with another guest. Please let me stay until they leave."

A look of irritation crossed Brad's face. "Praycash, you don't seem to get it. I, too, have challenges. But . . . here's a deal. I'll work with you if you can do something for us."

"Sure, I'll be happy to, Brad! I truly appreciate it."

"Good. Can you be Uncle Sam?"

"Excuse me?" Prakash wondered if he'd heard correctly.

Brad chuckled, for the first time. "Let me show you," he said, rising to go to the adjoining room. Moments later, returning with a box, he pulled out a red-white-blue striped outfit that included an elongated, matching hat.

Prakash was still puzzled. Without speaking, Brad took out what appeared to be a sign. ***"Great Deals at Sunrise Apartments . . . First Month Free!"*** it read. Prakash remained silent, waiting for him to say something. Instead, Brad pulled out another sign, shaped like a big arrow, and held it aloft.

"Fall Specials on Fully Furnished Apartments . . . Falling Rents!"

Then it struck home. Brad wanted him to don the Uncle Sam costume and be a sales promoter. For Sunrise Apartments! He was expected to walk up and down the nearby streets, twirling the signs, and catch the attention of motorists, some of whom—presumably—would be intrigued enough to stop and check out the rental offers.

Astonished, Prakash was slow to react. "Okay, now I understand," he finally said, nodding.

"So, can you do it, Praycash? I have another costume. But it's Lady Liberty . . . I don't think it will suit you. The Uncle Sam costume includes a fake beard, but that's optional." Chuckling again, he added, "Listen, I'll understand if you're not keen. Not everybody is comfortable with it. Just a thought. This is part of our fall marketing strategy . . . we're trying to attract more tenants. If you can do it, we'll take care of the rent for now."

Prakash said yes before he could change his mind. As he wore the loose-fitting costume over his clothes, the phone rang, drawing Brad's attention. Cradling the handset, as he spoke to a tenant, Brad smiled and gave Prakash a thumbs-up.

Emerging from the office, his gait a little awkward, Prakash decided to start at the far end of the complex and work his way to the street closest to his apartment. The hat, especially, felt ridiculous when he stepped on the sidewalk and saw the traffic flowing down the street. Wondering if anybody was laughing or pointing at him, he forced himself to not look at the passengers when the cars slowed or stopped at the lights. At first the signs remained frozen in his arms, as if he didn't know what to do. Prakash remembered, shamefacedly, how he sometimes caught himself staring at oddly dressed sign holders, as they walked or gyrated near intersections and in front of shopping plazas. How unfortunate, he'd think, that they had to settle for this unpleasant job.

Slowly, Prakash began to lose his inhibition, although he still avoided looking directly at the people driving by. Holding the signs up, Prakash swayed and turned, making sure the words were clearly visible. His attempt at twirling was less successful. A sign slipped and fell, to his embarrassment—and though nobody else seemed to care, Prakash decided he was not ready for twirling. Moving to another street, he wondered how Brad would know if this strategy was working. It was going to take time, no doubt. Would Brad ask prospective renters how they came to know about these specials?

Prakash thought he should be more dramatic to draw attention, that he should look at people and jab his finger towards Sunrise Apartments. But it wasn't easy. Maybe a mask would have helped. On occasion he had seen sign holders—their faces not visible—dressed up as Disney characters, bears, even *Sesame Street* characters. Why did Sunrise opt for Uncle Sam and Lady Liberty, anyway? Prakash would have asked Brad that question, but he felt the timing was inappropriate. Now, thinking it over, he could see a plausible explanation. Most of the tenants at Sunrise were new immigrants or visa holders, which meant that well-known American symbols like Uncle Sam and Lady Liberty would resonate more with people who had recently moved here from other countries.

Reaching the sidewalk near his apartment, Prakash paused. There were no pedestrians now. Still, he hesitated. The sun was out but not sharp, keeping the weather cool, and a gentle breeze prevented him from sweating. Without lowering the sign, Prakash resumed walking—only to stop in shock when he saw Chitra and his mother coming towards him. What were they doing here? Alarmed, he wondered if anything was wrong, but then realized they were actually strolling in the neighborhood, perhaps because they'd felt cooped up in the apartment.

Spinning around, Prakash kept his head down and walked fast, almost breaking into a run. They saw him, of course. But did they recognize him in this costume? Unlikely—for wouldn't they have called out his name? Nevertheless, Chitra seemed puzzled. Or was he imagining it? What he needed to do was get away, keep moving in the other direction.

Rounding the corner at the intersection, Prakash decided to cross the street even before the lights changed. There wasn't much traffic. Stepping off the curb, he didn't notice a car hurtling towards him—until it was too late. Then, in a moment of horror and terror, Prakash saw that he was going to be mowed down, annihilated in the prime of his life. But the driver's amazing reflexes, as Prakash later realized, led to a miraculous escape, with the car screeching to a halt just inches from his paralyzed body.

The driver got out, shaken and quaking with anger. "Watch where you're going, moron!" he shouted, gesticulating wildly. "Do you want to get killed?"

Though stunned by this close call, Prakash managed to apologize and move swiftly out of the way, just as an irate motorist behind the stationary car honked, forcing the driver back into his seat. Soon, the traffic resumed. Without looking back even once, Prakash held the hat in his arm and walked briskly to his car and unlocked the door. He was calm now. Leaving the window open to let in fresh air, he sat quietly and mulled things over. What he felt, above all, was overwhelming relief. A miraculous escape, and it felt like a turning point. And though he didn't know what lay in the future, he knew there would be no more deception or denial now.

Equanimity. The word came to him suddenly, echoing in his mind. He liked the sound of it. Prakash would face the road ahead with equanimity. After returning the costume to Brad, he'd transfer the money from his savings account and write a check for the payment he owed. And then, a cup of tea would be nice, in the company of his mother and Chitra. Prakash also looked forward to a nice chat with Chitra, as he'd promised her that morning. He was so glad that she had come.

They would all have a great Diwali. The festivities in town would be worth checking out, and he'd also take them to the temple on the mountain. Unlike the previous year, he wouldn't be alone. It would be a grand celebration—with fun, laughter, food—reminding him of the good times he used to have on those occasions.

HOLI DAY IN AMERICA

When Rohan first saw the man, it was shortly before his first Holi in the U.S. He remembered that not because of his mother's call—his family hosted a Holi party every year—but because of what happened over the couple of days leading up to the festival of colors, which he'd always celebrated in India. Until now. Almost a year ago, Rohan and his parents had arrived in America on immigrant visas. For complicated reasons, mostly involving his father, Rohan's parents had gone back to their native country. But Rohan decided to stay and look for a job. For him, America represented a new beginning, a fresh start in life.

That morning, opening the blinds of his window, he saw the man standing near the dumpster behind his apartment building. What struck him was that he didn't throw anything in after lifting the lid; instead, the man appeared to be searching for something. It was an unexpected sight, and as he stood there with a green canvas bag slung over his shoulder, Rohan continued watching him from his apartment on the third floor. He had a stubbly face and his dark hair was disheveled, but he didn't seem like a homeless person. If Rohan had to guess, he was a down-on-his-luck migrant from the Indian subcontinent.

Indeed, what had caught his attention and held it wasn't so much that the man was rummaging in the dumpster. He had occasionally seen homeless people opening the lid to look for discarded items. But this man, Rohan strongly felt, had come to the U.S. from the subcontinent not long ago. Like him. He looked up—and Rohan, flustered, quickly stepped back, wondering if he'd seen him. When he glanced down again, the man was gone.

Rohan couldn't help thinking about him on his way to work that day. Had he come here with hopes and dreams and full of ambition, like so many other immigrants, only to lose his way. Rohan didn't think he'd see him again—but he did, the very next morning. Standing near the dumpster, the man looked up, almost as if he expected to see him at his window. Rohan moved away in embarrassment. This must be a routine he had somehow missed. And when he left the building, the man was still there, patiently waiting on the sidewalk. The apartment building, mostly occupied by students, immigrants and a few office workers, was on a side street that had a café, a laundromat, a convenience store and a fast-food restaurant. Not many people were about at this time.

"Good morning," the man said, smiling tentatively. "Are you from India?"

"Yes." Taken aback, Rohan became tongue-tied. There was an awkward pause. Fishing out a couple of dollar bills from his pocket, he thrust them into his hand and continued walking fast. The man spoke again, but Rohan was already too far away to hear him properly—or more accurately, he pretended not to hear him.

Ashamed by his reaction, Rohan didn't stop when he got to the end of the side street. His weekday routine was to board a bus there. But turning at the corner, he decided to walk all the way to the bank where he worked. The early spring morning was bracing, making the walk enjoyable, and he admired the yellow flowering shrubs—forsythias?—that were already in bloom. Now that the long dreary winter was over, thankfully, he would no longer have to trudge past sad-looking skeletal trees or avoid the cold weather and the snow. Of course, watching and even touching the snow had been a thrilling experience. However, like his apartment building's other residents, he was ready for warmer days. As he gathered from the phone call, his family in India was getting ready for their annual Holi party. Guests, including some from out of town, would come to the outdoor celebration in festive clothes—only to have them joyfully ruined by splashing colors, to the accompaniment of screams and laughter. The Holi jamboree would then continue indoors with music, delicious food, dancing.

Rohan had no plans for Holi this year. A few people he knew had invited him to an informal party, but he didn't want to go. The carousing at these gatherings, not to mention any remembrances of festivals past, could be disheartening, making people maudlin. Being in no mood for nostalgia, he also decided to skip the boxed sweets he bought for such occasions. He wanted to look ahead, not behind, at this point in his life.

As Rohan approached the bank, his thoughts shifted to that morning's strange encounter. Why had he walked away from the man so abruptly? Was it because the sight of an able-bodied immigrant—from India, no less—begging on the streets of America had unsettled him? True, he hadn't asked for money. But he did accept the dollar bills, didn't he?

Rohan's friend David felt he was supercilious—it was one of those words David sometimes liked to use. He was wrong. Rohan didn't look down on anybody; yet he did believe that anybody who could work should get a job, even if it was very humble, and not depend on handouts. The morning's encounter had unnerved him. To come to this country, willingly, and end up like this was a personal failing, wasn't it?

David would smile, not unkindly, when Rohan said that America was a land of opportunity for those who worked hard, regardless of their origin. It tickled him to hear Rohan go on about the "American dream," which David thought was a cliché. He pointed out that the "dream" only applied to folks who already had the advantages, not to those left behind in a brutally competitive market economy and a stratified society where factors like race, class and region still held sway. Speaking of clichés, David wasn't above using phrases like "winner-take-all," although Rohan had to admit that their discussions were always cordial.

Sometimes they went to a fast-food restaurant near the branch where Rohan worked as a customer service representative. David, widowed and retired from his teaching job, had invested in a bookstore that was in a converted house on the other side of the street. It seemed like a quixotic venture, and as far as Rohan could tell, the business wasn't making much money. They usually got apple pie and coffee at the fast-food restaurant.

"Take them, for instance," David once said, referring to the servers. "Do you think they get paid enough for what they do? Upbeat clichés mean very little to them."

"But David, that's where you're wrong. The opportunities are there if one is willing to make the right choices and work hard."

Putting his cup down, he snorted. "Look, who's talking! I don't mean to get personal, but given your professional qualifications, I think you should have a better-paying job."

"That was back home. Being a recent immigrant, the path is more challenging for me, David. I have to pay my dues—at least, that's how I see it. I made a conscious decision to come here, so I accept that. I was willing to give up certain advantages, because I knew there would be other advantages. But I'll achieve my goals one day."

"Hmm . . . I'm sure you will," David said, raising his cup. "You're a determined fellow. Despite being a recent immigrant, I'd say that you're more American than you realize."

For a moment Rohan assumed he was mocking him, but the smile on David's face was genial, not sarcastic, and it was tinged with admiration. Some people seemed to think Rohan was cocky, even boastful. They misunderstood him. There was a fellow in his apartment building, an older immigrant, with whom Rohan had struck up a friendship. He came across as hardworking and resilient—a feeling that was reinforced when Rohan heard a harrowing story about the man's encounter with a robber. However, as he got to know him better, Rohan realized that he liked to complain. He whined about discrimination. His ethnic background and beliefs impeded him from getting ahead, the man said. He belonged to the wrong minority. And in a race-and religion conscious country, there were limits to how far he could rise. America owed him nothing, Rohan wanted to say, because nobody had forced him to come here. It had accepted him, after all. But Rohan kept his thoughts to himself, not wanting to offend him or wade in the bog of identity politics. Becoming disenchanted, he began to avoid the man. Rohan had no use for, as he saw it, the cult of victimhood.

The morning after having coffee with David, a loud grinding noise wakened Rohan. A garbage truck was backing up for the weekly collection from the dumpster.

Later, as he was leaving the building to go to work, Rohan didn't see the man with the green canvas bag standing outside. He was disappointed rather than relieved, to be honest, and wondered if he'd ever see him again.

He got his answer that afternoon.

It was almost closing time, with only a couple of customers waiting in line, when the man walked into the branch. Rohan felt his stomach clench. His appearance was so unexpected—how did the man know where he worked?—that Rohan lost track of the bundle of cash he was counting. Being a small branch, his duties included helping with teller transactions, which at this hour before the weekend began usually meant cashing paychecks and, less often, taking deposits. The other teller, having completed her transactions, closed her window and started wrapping up. After the customer he was serving left, Rohan looked up and saw the man—with the same green canvas bag slung over his shoulder—standing quietly near the "Please Wait Here" sign. Again, he felt agitated. What did the man want? Was he really an account holder at the bank? Rohan struggled to shake off the suspicion clouding his mind.

The man was holding a piece of folded paper. Was it a menacing, hastily scrawled note? Rohan told himself that he shouldn't jump to conclusions, let his imagination run wild. After all, he hadn't even spoken yet. But then how did he know that Rohan worked here, unless he'd followed him? Or was this a coincidence? Rohan helped the next customer, and a few minutes later, the Mystery Man was the only outsider in the branch, making him the last customer—if that was the right word—for the day.

"May I help you, sir?" Rohan said.

"Yes . . . hello. You may remember me . . . we met yesterday. Would I be able to cash this foreign draft?"

His English was flawless and he spoke with the clear, educated accent of somebody who had studied at a good school. Recalling his behavior the previous day, Rohan cringed inwardly. The slightly crumpled draft was drawn on a bank in India. He wondered, fleetingly, if the man had received it from his family. The relief Rohan felt was tinged with guilt.

"We have to send it for collection, sir. Do you have an account with us?"

"No, I don't. Can you not do it if I pay the collection fee?"

"Our policy is to do it for bank customers, but please ask the manager there. She may be able to help you."

"That's fine," the man said, taking his draft back. "I'm expecting a money order. Maybe it will come tomorrow. You're closing now, anyway."

The manager, standing in the lobby, had locked the doors exactly at 5 p.m. Now she used her key to let him out. Rohan closed his window to complete the remaining tasks.

Leaving the bank, he wondered if David was still in the bookstore. Earlier, when he had an assistant, whose duties included online sales, the store used to be open for a good part of the day. But after the employee left for another job, David stopped maintaining regular hours.

It was during a lunch break, shortly after he'd started working at the bank, that Rohan paid his first visit to the bookstore. Its intriguing sign—Leaf and Loaf—had drawn him. Sitting behind the counter, with just his cat for company, David was packing some books. The calm, almost monastic silence contrasted with the ceaseless bustle outside, making the store, despite its mustiness, cozy and welcoming. After wandering past rows of books stacked high on groaning shelves, Rohan selected a decade-old hardback that was in mint condition and headed to the counter. Although the book looked untouched, David informed him with a smile how much he'd enjoyed reading it years ago. Soon, they started chatting about Asia—particularly India, which David had crisscrossed as a young man.

That memory of his first visit to Leaf and Loaf came back to Rohan as he walked towards the bookstore. It was still open.

"Glad to see you," David said, looking up from a box that he'd just finished packing. "Something unexpected just happened. An interesting young man walked into the store a short while ago. And guess what? He's from India!"

"Really?"

"He had a recent setback, which he wasn't too anxious to talk about. But we did talk about books. He is impressively knowledgeable. I offered him a job."

"You did what?" Rohan was stunned.

"Well, as you know, I need help if I'm going to keep the store open for longer hours. And I'm not very good with online sales and social media. He's okay with the fact that I can't pay him much, at least initially. Let's see how it works out."

Rohan didn't tell David about his encounter with the man in the branch, or ask him for a description of his new assistant. Who else could it be?

"Wonderful, David," he said, shaking his hand. "I'm happy to hear the news."

"Listen, I know you're off tomorrow. Do you have plans for Holly? Or is it Holy something? Sorry if I'm mispronouncing it. You'd mentioned that festival last time. If you're free, how about stopping by? You can meet him, and maybe we can have a mini celebration."

Rohan was stumped, but only for a moment. "Sure, that sounds great, David. I have no plans for Holi."

As Rohan said goodbye, he made a mental note to pick up a box of sweets.

IN THE NEW WORLD

"I'm here only because of my daughter," he said, not looking up as he closed the menu.

Amar had already said that a few times—using the same words, in fact—but he was obviously reminding me, as if he knew why I had invited him to lunch. It seemed like he wanted to deflect any criticism of him. Or perhaps he was seeking reassurance.

"Of course," I said, "it doesn't surprise me. I'm sure your daughter appreciates it. You gave up a good career, a good life—"

"Don't get me wrong." He raised his head, his eyes widening under his bushy eyebrows. "I'm not saying I made a big sacrifice. I came because we wanted to move here. But, you know, it's not easy being a new immigrant at my age . . . not easy to be jobless, face uncertainty."

He was being dramatic. Amar had been offered a retail position, but according to his wife, he rejected it because of the low pay and status. An earlier job had lasted only a few days—or rather, nights—because, as he put it, staying awake when everybody else was sleeping was not for him. I wondered if he'd been fired. He'd reportedly worked at another place afterwards, but that job had been short-lived as well. And then he did something bizarre, alarming his wife.

Calling me one day on my cellphone, as I was returning to the office after lunch, she told me about it. A resident in their building had seen Amar near the ramp of a busy highway, holding a sign that read: "Experienced engineer and operations manager seeks work commensurate with qualifications."

Furious and concerned, she demanded an explanation when her husband got home. He jokingly said that one had to use creative methods to find a proper job. When she threatened to move out, Amar quickly backed off and said that he'd done this only a couple of times, briefly. He wouldn't do it again. In any case, motorists seemed to think it was a prank.

Flabbergasted, I didn't know what to say. Was he losing it? This was her second phone call to me, and I wondered how Amar would react if he found out that she was calling me. While she was practical and resourceful, he came across as a dreamer with unrealistic expectations. She had no qualms about working long hours at a supermarket, which offered health insurance for the family and provided job security. But it wasn't easy, and her husband's vacillation frustrated her.

"Please talk to him," she implored. "You're one of the few people here he knows and trusts. He'll come to his senses if he listens to you."

I was doubtful, though I didn't say so. My wife, to be honest, didn't much care for Amar and thought he was cocky and irresponsible. But she liked Amar's wife and offered her help when they were settling in. My wife hadn't disagreed with my point that Amar was complicated, and she understood my desire to be involved in his life, even if we weren't really friends and I hadn't known him personally back in India. She had a generous side, but her focus was more on volunteering locally and making contributions to local causes. It was noble, and sometimes I felt I should be more like her. There were any number of worthy mainstream initiatives, as she pointed out, and I could pick one that appealed to me.

Nevertheless, I was an immigrant, unlike my wife, and I still found myself drawn to the old world. Did it involve some guilt? Perhaps, though I didn't see it that way. My interests had a lot to do with a circle of friends I had cultivated—friends who felt we should do more for the country we'd left behind. So we pooled our resources to help a foundation that promoted children's education, and we became active participants in events—such as walkathons and concerts—to raise funds and awareness. I was a classic first-generation immigrant, I suppose, caught between two worlds; I'd embraced the new world, and was even married to a woman from here, but I still had a foot in the old world. My children, I knew, would be different.

Immigrants, my wife once remarked, probably wouldn't be as deeply involved in each other's lives if it hadn't been for the bond created by their shared journey. True, I said, especially when those immigrants—like me—came from a culture that was more traditional, more group-oriented.

Coming back to Amar, I'd already shared his resume with prospective employers, made calls on his behalf, and given him tips and leads. I even provided a reference. He got some responses, but nothing solid had panned out yet. Telling him to be patient, I'd asked him to accept, just as his wife had, a lower-paying retail job until something better came along. If retail wasn't his cup of tea, there were other possibilities. Amar wasn't enthusiastic, so I decided to leave him alone for a while and let him find his way. He was a grown man, after all.

Of course, that's not what Amar's wife wanted to hear. Without interrupting her, I entered my building and, holding the phone, climbed the stairs to my office. I'd stopped using the elevator, seeing the stairs as a good opportunity for getting exercise on weekdays.

Only last night, she continued, her husband had said he was ready to go back, ready to give up on his American dream. He missed his old life, but didn't expect her or their daughter to accompany him. Amar would return to India alone. Once he was established—which shouldn't take long, according to him—he'd send money. His needs were few. With her help, they'd be able to put their daughter through college.

In a plaintive voice, she added, "It's crazy. I don't know what's happened to him."

I was nonplussed. Then, finding my voice, I mumbled some soothing words and said I'd be happy to talk to him soon over lunch at a restaurant.

"The prices here are high," Amar said, looking around nervously at the other diners. "We should have gone to the buffet place I was telling you about."

"Come on, Amar, I already said this was my treat. Easier to talk here. The buffet place gets crowded—and frankly, the food here is much better." I was glad we'd managed to snag a corner booth that gave us some privacy.

He nodded glumly and, without looking at the menu again, said he'd have whatever I was ordering. I didn't know what to make of him. I wasn't trying to downplay the struggles of new immigrants, but Amar had been such a go-getter that it was astonishing to see the transformation. A quarter-century ago, he'd been one of the brightest students in his class, known not only for his ambition but also for his commitment to the arts, especially music. Strangely, though he had been active in the concert scene, both on and off campus, I couldn't remember what instrument he used to play. Being younger, I had joined the same college after him. We had never spoken back then. But my cousin had been his classmate and it was because of him that Amar got in touch with me after he moved to the U.S.

Amar's shoulders stooped as he sat. Despite his hangdog appearance and thinning grey hair, one could tell that he wasn't a dour—or old—man. His face was still unlined, and he'd shed some pounds in recent weeks, giving him a leaner look. Amar only had to smile, which I hoped he'd do more often, to reveal a sunnier, livelier side.

Before meeting him, I learned through my cousin that, prior to his move to the U.S., Amar had risen swiftly through the ranks in the corporate world, attaining a respectable position. But something had changed. Sure, moving to a new country can be challenging. And yet, on our first meeting, soon after his arrival, he'd been upbeat and full of energy. The possibilities for his family seemed rich and he was very hopeful about his prospects.

So what happened—why had things gone downhill that quickly? He was dejected, even depressed. Years ago, my cousin said, people had spoken well of him, seeing him as an up-and-coming young man with a bright future. And indeed, in his old life, Amar had to a large extent fulfilled those expectations. In his new life, though, he seemed lost, reminding me of a man who slumbers for so long that when he wakes, unexpectedly, he's bewildered by all the changes around him. It's a new era, the unfamiliar rules and customs making him a stranger. Moving to a new country can change everything, I suppose. Amar hadn't found his bearings—yet.

Paying the bill, I realized we weren't talking about what Amar was going to do, how he was going to make progress. Our conversation was desultory. As we drifted from topic to topic, I avoided bringing up the topic that was uppermost in my mind. His demeanor and subdued manner discouraged me from asking intrusive questions. I didn't want to come across as a busybody. Bringing him to this restaurant had been a mistake, only reminding him of his diminished status. It was too fancy. I thought it would be a nice change, but I had miscalculated.

Now, as we walked out, I couldn't think of anything to say. Pep talks and platitudes seemed pointless when, as his wife put it, he was so "proud" that he wouldn't settle for a modest job. Looking for a suitable position in his field demanded his full attention, he'd told her, leaving him little time for other work. But Amar had nothing to show for it, and she was getting tired of his shenanigans. How long could they continue like this?

"Amar, I haven't been to your apartment," I said, opening my car door. "Let me drop you there."

"What's there to see? It's a shabby apartment in a shabby building." He laughed mirthlessly. "Sometimes, before I open my front door, I'm greeted by a bag of dog poo."

"Did you complain?" I said, shocked.

Smiling, he shook his head, and by the look on his face I could tell he thought I was clueless. I had a good, well-paying job and my family led a comfortable life in an attractive, secure neighborhood where we owned a house. What did I know about his trials—such as the bigotry and uncertainty he had to face in this bewildering country, which he was finding so hard to decipher and get ahead in?

For me, however, Amar was hard to decipher. He seemed both proud and needy, presenting a curious mix of arrogance and vulnerability. His struggle to live with diminished expectations and status was painfully obvious. Had he suffered other indignities that he was unwilling to share? I was sympathetic, but I knew an attitude adjustment would help him enormously. I just didn't know how to convey that without offending him.

"Well, I'll see you," he said. "Thanks for the lunch. I'll let you get back to work. I can walk from here . . . it's not far. Let's meet again."

"No worries, Amar. I know you don't want me to drop you, but I'll tell you something before we part. Your wife called me a couple of times."

Amar stared at me. When I saw his face turn red—in embarrassment, certainly, but perhaps also in anger—I was filled with regret for being so impulsive. Was he going to berate her for calling me?

"She's worried," I continued. "We feel you're drifting—and need help. She turned to me out of desperation."

"Oh, did she?" Amar's voice dropped. He seemed deflated. Perhaps what I said didn't surprise him, and he'd already figured out that his wife had instigated the meeting.

"I think we should talk more, Amar, maybe over tea. I don't have anything pressing at the office. Your wife can join us if she's interested."

"She's at the store now, but come to the apartment," Amar said unexpectedly. "You can have tea there. My daughter and wife will be home by four."

We didn't talk as I drove, and since the traffic was fairly light at this time of day, it didn't take long to reach Amar's neighborhood. I found a parking spot on the littered street, which had a few potholes and was lined with grimy, graffiti-scarred buildings. Not many people were about. Although Amar's apartment building looked gloomy, it was in better shape than the other buildings in the area. Opening the creaky front door, we entered a narrow passage.

"The lift . . . elevator . . . broke down again," Amar said. "Let's take the stairs."

It was a little dank and dingy inside, with stained walls, and the building was unnaturally quiet. But then we heard the loud, monotonous siren of a fire truck as it went down the street. When we reached the third floor, Amar took out his key and unlocked the apartment door.

"No dog poo today," he said, entering. "So that's good news."

"Why don't you move out? I know it's an expensive city, but if you keep looking, there are possibilities—"

"Yes, we've thought about it. We didn't know any better, but the school is decent. Our lease won't expire until next year."

The modest apartment, furnished with mismatched items that seemed to have been bought at thrift stores, was neatly kept and not uninviting. If I had to guess, it was Amar's wife who had turned this place into a home, a welcome refuge for the family in this dreary, crumbling neighborhood.

"Have a seat," Amar said, gesturing at the most comfortable chair, which was near a worn sofa that had lumpy yellow cushions. "I'll make some tea."

There was, directly across from the well-padded armchair I was sitting in, what looked like a wooden television stand. But instead of a television set, what I saw was a tabla set, with the two drums resting on a bottle green tablecloth. It triggered a memory.

Men Tal. Amar's music group was called Men Tal—*tal*, I knew, referred to meter in classical music—and it had four male performers. He played the tabla, one was a vocalist, and the other two played string instruments. Although I'd never seen them perform, I knew they'd been well regarded by aficionados. As a teenager, I'd seen a flier promoting their concert, which my cousin and a few other people I knew had attended—and liked. The group had even made an album.

While Men Tal lasted only a few years, Amar had apparently kept up with his music. When he returned with the tea, I pointed at the tabla and said that his commitment to music was commendable, given his current situation. And here, I added, he was deprived of an audience, not just the monetary compensation. Passion was the fuel that seemed to keep him going.

Chortling, he handed me a cup before sitting on the sofa.

"Keeps me sane, but it makes the guy downstairs insane," he said. "That's why we get presents like dog poo. But I'm very careful. I play it only for a limited time in the afternoon when there are few people in the building."

I was tempted to ask him to play for me now. First, however, I had to tell him something important. "Amar, here's an opportunity for you. My son takes lessons at a music school that's looking for more instructors. They're growing and doing well. I'm sure they don't have a tabla player. They'd love to have somebody like you . . . somebody of your caliber."

"Really?" His eyes lit up. "Sounds interesting. Is the school close to your house?"

"Not far," I said, resting the cup on my lap. "It's accessible for you because there's a station nearby. It won't take you more than thirty minutes by train. I'll be glad to talk to them."

Amar put his cup on the floor. Then, in a gesture that surprised and touched me, he folded his hands and did a little bow.

THE MISSING HUSBAND

"Come to my apartment this evening and meet Kalpana," Dilip said, smiling. "We can have dinner. My wife and you have something in common."

Shankar was in the convenience store near their apartment building that morning, paying for a carton of milk and the Sunday newspaper, when Dilip walked in and unexpectedly tapped him on the shoulder. Dilip's relaxed, cheerful manner contrasted with his generally somber mood, and as he stood there talking, Shankar couldn't help thinking that his wife's arrival from India had affected his demeanor. Just a week ago, in their somewhat rickety elevator, he'd nervously told Shankar he was on his way to the airport to pick up Kalpana.

Now there was an amiable calmness about him that Shankar hadn't noticed before. His invitation was also surprising because, although they'd known each other for over a year, they weren't really friends. Although they spoke cordially to each other, in the building or outside, Dilip's reserved manner, which Shankar attributed to shyness or perhaps the breakup of his first marriage, discouraged him from being more forthcoming. The tenants in their building—mostly immigrants of various nationalities—formed a motley group: young families, students, middle-aged couples, retirees, and single people with jobs in the surrounding area. This multistory home, fully occupied and often buzzing with activity, had a multicultural ambience that was attractive and Shankar found the anonymity it provided reassuring. He thought of it as a mini UN.

Dilip lived on the sixth floor and Shankar's apartment was on the third. Given that their conversations seldom progressed beyond casual pleasantries, Dilip wasn't the source of everything Shankar knew about him. It was Nadia, the gregarious superintendent of their apartment building, who had once told Shankar that Dilip's ex-wife and child lived on the West Coast and that his marriage to Kalpana had been arranged in India.

Punctually at seven that evening, Shankar showed up at their door with a bottle of wine. In the store that morning, Dilip had intrigued him with his comment that Kalpana and he had something in common. But without elaborating, and grinning enigmatically, he'd reminded him to come at seven and hurried off to get his grocery items. Now that was the first thing Shankar thought of as soon as he walked into their living room and saw her. The mystery was soon solved when Dilip, smiling broadly, informed him that his wife and Shankar had grown up in the same town. Dressed elegantly in a crimson sari, her long and wavy dark hair hanging loose, Kalpana seemed considerably younger than her husband, and as she came forward to greet him, exuding a pleasing fragrance, Shankar wondered if he'd seen her before. She looked vaguely familiar.

"Kalpana and you attended the same college in India," Dilip said, startling him.

Shankar didn't think he'd mentioned his alma mater to Dilip, but he must have said something in passing, obviously, and was touched that he still remembered. Smiling warmly, she didn't add anything. Although Kalpana remained at ease during Shankar's visit, he could sense that she was still adjusting to her new environment; after all, she'd arrived just a week ago. And judging by her friendly manner, she seemed glad to see him. Eventually, when they were chatting about their hometown and alma mater, Shankar realized that it was actually Kalpana's older sister he'd seen in India. They'd been students around the same time—and apparently, she bore a resemblance to Kalpana. Having made only occasional visits to India, Shankar was eager to learn about the latest developments back home.

What he remembered most clearly about that first meeting was the way Kalpana's matching red earrings glittered in the fluorescent light as she sat on the sofa, talking and smiling. Dilip had ordered food from an Indian restaurant close by, and the inviting aroma of the dishes added to the homey setting. Sitting near his wife, Dilip listened attentively as Kalpana and Shankar reminisced about their college days. As she spoke about her family, with a dreamy look on her face, Shankar's mood became a little melancholic as well, and at one point—obviously homesick—Kalpana became quiet and turned her face away. But she swiftly pulled herself together. Before long, to the accompaniment of softly playing Indian film music, they were having dinner at the table. When Shankar left not long afterwards, Dilip walked with him down the long passage to the elevator.

"Kalpana misses her family," he said, pressing the button. "I'm happy you could come. It cheered her up."

"My pleasure . . . " Shankar was at a loss for words.

Clink-Clank . . . Clink-Clank . . . Clink-Clank . . . PING!

Dilip smiled wanly as the elevator noisily announced its arrival. "Please come again," he added. "Kalpana will like that. She doesn't have any friends here yet. And I travel a lot—"

"Yes," Shankar managed to say before the elevator doors closed.

This expression of friendship and trust was certainly flattering, considering that they didn't know each other well. Dilip probably felt that his wife would feel comfortable with Shankar, and even enjoy his company, because of their shared background. It was an odd remark, though, and Shankar was baffled.

He was busy at work the next few days, but after completing his project on Friday, Shankar decided to invite Dilip and Kalpana for a casual get-together over the weekend. Rising early on Saturday, he thought he'd do a few chores first and call Dilip later in the morning. The apartment building's coin-operated laundry machines were on the tenth floor. Holding his basket of clothes, he got off the elevator and walked past strangely silent apartments to the last room, where he didn't expect to see anybody at this hour. Near the entrance, he caught a glimpse of the gently drifting snow through a large window. It was the first shower of the season, and in the calmness of the morning, with many of the tenants still asleep, this enchanting view of what looked like fluffy cotton balls floating in the air had a hypnotic effect on him.

Then he saw Kalpana.

Standing in a corner, she was gazing at the snowfall, but then, sensing Shankar's presence, she turned her head. Approaching her, he was startled to see that her cheeks were moist. There was an awkward moment, and feeling that he was intruding, Shankar almost swung around to leave the room. But Kalpana smiled and said hello. Her clothes were churning in a dryer close by.

"This weather must be a big change for you," he said. "Getting used to it takes a while."

"Yes, but the snow looks very pretty from up here." Then, unexpectedly, she asked, "How well do you know Dilip?"

Though taken aback, he immediately said, "Not very well, but we've known each other casually for over a year."

"That's what I thought." She opened the dryer to pick up her clothes.

"Did you know that Dilip was previously married?"

"Yes . . . but we really didn't talk about it—"

A couple of tenants entered the room, abruptly ending their conversation. Having gathered her clothes, Kalpana smiled goodbye and walked out. Wondering if something had happened between Dilip and Kalpana, Shankar decided to postpone his invitation to the next day. He was puzzled by her comment at first, then alarmed. Yet he didn't want to make hasty assumptions about their relationship. Returning from another errand that afternoon, he ran into Nadia. Pulling him aside, she seemed eager to ask him something.

"Have you heard anything from Kalpana?" she said in a low voice.

"No," he said. "What do you mean?"

"Didn't you know? Her husband is missing."

"Missing?"

The shocked expression on Shankar's face must have unsettled her, for she hastily added, "What I mean is that Dilip left two or three days ago without informing her. She asked if I'd heard from him. That's all. I don't know if he contacted her afterwards—"

Clink-Clank . . . Clink-Clank . . . Clink-Clank . . . PING!

When the elevator doors opened to disgorge a few people, Nadia nodded at him and hurried off to her next task. Acting on an impulse, Shankar took the elevator up to the sixth floor and, walking over to Dilip's apartment, hesitantly rang the doorbell. Opening the door, Kalpana seemed surprised to see him. But not annoyed, he hoped. Her eyes, he noticed, were a little red, as if she'd been crying.

"Just dropped by . . . to say hello," he said. "Any news from Dilip?"

There was an awkward pause.

"Did you see a 'Missing Husband' flier in the lobby?" she finally said, breaking into a grim smile.

"Flier?" He was bewildered and his face turned red. "No . . . no . . . I just spoke to Nadia."

"I know. I'm sorry . . . it was a feeble joke. Yes, Dilip did call me."

Shankar wondered if they'd had a big quarrel before he left. Did she make a disturbing discovery about him? More specifically, was he still married to another woman? It was an appalling thought, of course, but he remembered her questions in the laundry room and realized that he couldn't dismiss such a possibility.

"Is everything okay, Kalpana?" he said, reaching out unthinkingly to touch her arm. "Let me know if I can do anything." His behavior seemed presumptuous to him even as he was saying those words, but Kalpana didn't withdraw her arm.

"Yes, Shankar, thank you," she said. "I know that I can count on you. For now, please let me deal with it. I'll call you if I need anything." Then, after giving his arm a gentle squeeze, she released it and stepped back into the apartment.

Kalpana did call one day, but only to say goodbye. Returning late to his apartment, Shankar found a short message from her on his answering machine. Informing him that she was leaving that afternoon to join her husband, Kalpana added that he shouldn't worry about her. "I appreciate your concern and kindness," she said. "We can talk once things are back to normal."

For a while Shankar seriously thought about trying to contact her. Nadia probably had her new phone number or forwarding address. But then, realizing that Kalpana most likely wished to be left alone, he decided to wait. All indications were that she wanted to keep her dilemma a secret and deal with it on her own. Shankar brooded over it but made no attempt to gather more information, and not long afterwards, he got busy with his own life when he started a new job. He purchased a condominium and, around the same time, began dating a former colleague. The relationship didn't last, but they parted on good terms and remained in touch. As Shankar settled into a routine in his new neighborhood, which was in another section of the city, he stopped going to the places he used to frequent.

Then one Saturday afternoon, months later, he decided to visit his old neighborhood and, if possible, say hello to Nadia. It was cold again and as he walked towards the apartment building on that wind-swept street, the blowing snow reminded him of the day he'd seen Kalpana in the laundry room. It was hard to believe that a year had passed by. Was she still living with Dilip on the West Coast? As he approached those familiar glass doors, the thought of another long and dreary winter made him a little disconsolate, but he perked up when he saw Nadia's cheerful face. Greeting him effusively, she began to chat as usual and even offered a cup of hot tea, which Shankar gratefully accepted. Not surprisingly, Nadia did have some news.

"Kalpana came here not long ago to take care of a few things," she said. "You know, she divorced Dilip."

Becoming still, Shankar couldn't think of anything to say. They were back in the lobby by now and he was about to leave. A resident who was returning to the building opened the front door, letting in an icy blast of air. Shivering slightly, he could see that it was still blustery as the snow continued to come down.

"Do you know what happened between them?" he finally asked, lowering his voice.

"Dilip and a few other people at his former company got into trouble," she said, coming closer. "Corporate fraud, I think. After they had the evidence, he was arrested here."

"Did Kalpana know?" Trying to absorb the information, he wondered how Nadia knew these details.

"Not at first. Kalpana told me all this when she came here. Initially she thought it was another woman. Dilip tried to hide the news from her, insisting that he was being framed. She found out the truth later. By the way, Kalpana asked about you."

"Really?" Shankar said, feeling his chest tighten.

"Yes, I told her about the condo and your girlfriend." Nadia laughed. "I gave her your phone number. Didn't she—?"

"Do you have her phone number? Do you know where she lives?"

"She did give me her new address, but I'll have to look for it and get back to you. Kalpana also said that she'd be going to India for a while."

There was nothing more to keep him there. Thanking her and saying that he'd be in touch again, Shankar stepped outside. The snow-borne wind felt like a cold slap on his face, making him wince. Lowering his head against the bitter onslaught of the worsening weather, he walked briskly towards the subway station. Rising late after a restless night, when the wind had howled intermittently and rattled the windows, he prepared his usual Sunday breakfast of omelet and buttered toast, which he washed down with a pot of coffee. By now the wind had died down and only flakes were drifting down, but the ground was already thickly carpeted with snow, and in the ghostly stillness of a chilly morning, the bare trees shimmering outside were like white sculptures in a deserted winter garden.

Nadia called that evening to tell him that she'd found Kalpana's contact information. Surprisingly, it turned out to be the address for an apartment complex near the local university.

"There's no phone number because, as I remember now, Kalpana is moving in after she returns from India next week," Nadia said. "In fact, she jotted down her flight number and the date of arrival on this piece of paper. Let me read it to you."

A few days later, leaving his office a little early, Shankar drove directly to the airport. He hadn't planned to do so, and on reaching the baggage claim area, his misgivings returned. Observing the travelers as they streamed towards the conveyer belts, which were revolving in endless loops, he wondered how Kalpana would react to his unexpected appearance. With surprise, surely, but would she be dipleased? He hoped not, considering that she'd asked Nadia for his phone number. What should he say? All he had in mind at that moment was a desire to get in touch with her, though he knew it was an odd—or bizarre—way to do it.

Dressed in jeans and a beige pullover, Kalpana had blended in with the surging crowd, but because of her distinctive mass of black hair, now tied in a ponytail, he could recognize her even from a distance. He was about to move towards her as she approached the baggage carousel, when she abruptly turned around to greet somebody. Within seconds, a smiling young man caught up with her and placed his hand on her arm. They laughed, perhaps over some shared experience. Then, along with the other passengers, they began looking for their baggage. Suddenly feeling awkward, Shankar walked away without greeting her.

The following evening, just as he was finishing his dinner, the phone rang. It was Kalpana.

"Shankar, I wanted to call you after Nadia gave me your phone number," she said. "But then I ended up going to India. I returned yesterday."

"Nadia gave me your address and I was planning to get in touch with you," he said. "It was nice to know that you'd be living here again."

"Yes, I'm happy about it. I've enrolled in a graduate program at the university. My classes begin next week."

"That's wonderful, Kalpana. I wish you all the best. Now that you're back, we should get together sometime."

"Absolutely. In fact, that's why I called you. We should definitely get together soon. I felt bad about cutting you off—"

"No, Kalpana, don't say that. I understand. It was a difficult period for you."

"Yes, Shankar . . . thankfully, it's over now. Did Nadia tell you what happened?"

"Briefly. I'm sorry you had to go through that."

Kalpana didn't elaborate except to say that, being "finally free" to get on with her life, she was excited about continuing her education. Since she'd be busy settling in over the weekend, they agreed to meet on a weekday afternoon at a café near the campus.

Popular among students, the café was crowded when Shankar arrived, but soon a table near the window became available. Walking in before long, Kalpana took off her coat and pulled up a chair. They were, it appeared, greeting each other like old friends. Dressed casually, and carrying a bag stuffed with books and papers, she seemed completely at home in her new environment. Her easygoing, confident manner was so striking that it was hard to believe she'd been married to Dilip. His name did not come up even once. Normal conversation proved to be difficult in the noisy café, but in any case, as Kalpana apologetically explained, she couldn't stay for long because of an unanticipated meeting scheduled in her department. Shankar barely sipped his coffee while they talked, mostly about the classes she was taking and her trip to India.

"I'm glad you could make it today," she said. "It was nice to see you again, Shankar. Before I leave, I'd like you to meet somebody."

Raising his head in surprise, Shankar saw the young man he'd seen with her at the airport. Smiling as before, he was approaching their table. He had entered the café earlier, Shankar could tell, since he was holding a steaming paper cup as they shook hands and exchanged pleasantries. He, too, was from their hometown in India and he'd enrolled in the same graduate program as Kalpana. Fleetingly, Shankar wondered if they shared her new apartment near the university. And more tantalizingly, he wondered if they'd known each other before she got married to Dilip.

Sitting again after they left, Shankar picked up his cup, though what he craved was fresh coffee. But there was a line at the counter and he didn't want to wait; it was time for him to head back to his office. It hadn't snowed much since the day he'd visited Nadia, and now with the sun shining brightly, the weather seemed spring-like. That was deceptive. Gazing through the window, he knew it would remain chilly for a while. Watching Kalpana and the young man walk towards the campus, Shankar swallowed the rest of his coffee, which had by now become cold and rather flavorless.

THE VISITOR AND THE NEIGHBOR

That morning, for the first time since he landed in the U.S., Prasad does not acknowledge his son's greeting. Although awake, he remains quiet when Vijay, stopping by the closed door as usual, knocks and says, "Good morning, Papa." Pause. Getting no response, Vijay drops the newspaper on the floor and walks away briskly, his footsteps resounding in the hallway. Every morning for about three weeks, Prasad has been opening the door to return his son's greeting and take the paper from him. But not today.

Reluctant to get out of bed, Prasad listens to the sounds of the household. Doors open; patter on the staircase; chatter in the kitchen; plates clatter; the microwave hums. The morning routine reaches a climax with the rumble of the garage door, whose rapid descent sounds like the closing of a prison gate. Prasad once heard a friend say, with a laugh, that when he was visiting his daughter in America, her suburban home had felt like "a five-star jail" after she went to work. He didn't know anybody else there, and couldn't go anywhere without her—but every comfort he could think of was readily available.

Prasad's daughter-in-law, Uma, who has a longer commute, is the first person to leave the house. Then it is Vijay's turn, and he leaves for his office with their daughter, Mala, whom he drops off at school on the way. Having quickly eaten their breakfast in the kitchen, they exit through the side door leading to the garage. And then comes the silence that seems to have sneaked in through the same door, even at the same time, like a taciturn cellmate.

Prasad switches on the radio next to his bed, and a reporter's excited prattle fills the room. What happened to the sprightly music he used to hear on this station? Now that everybody has left the house, he feels guilty that he ignored his son. But it couldn't be helped. Following the previous day's incident, Prasad wanted a break—and so, rather than face Vijay and relive the embarrassing moment, he pretended to be asleep. Rising now, he gets ready and makes a cup of coffee using the Keurig machine. How easy this is compared to what he's used to, he marvels, as the coffeemaker gurgles and the brew's rich aroma fills his nostrils. After finishing his yoga routine, Prasad picks up the paper—but today he is unable to concentrate.

Switching off the radio, whose nonstop chatter has begun to grate, he paces back and forth in the empty house, going from the front door to the back door that leads to the yard. A few rounds later, still feeling restless, he steps outside through the front door. But he's not going to walk in the neighborhood, as he used to. While his son hasn't placed any restrictions, he did gently suggest that Prasad would be better off sticking close to the house. So from now, until he heads back to India, he'll only walk on the property.

The throbbing sound of a lawn mower draws his attention. Walking towards it, he sees Vijay's neighbor, Ethan Cooper, pushing the mower in his front yard. Prasad is, once again, struck by the old man's energy. And what about his clothes—or rather, his shorts? Prasad has never worn shorts as an adult. As for yard maintenance, his son hardly does anything on his own, having outsourced the job to a landscaping company. But here's this neighbor, who seems to be about Prasad's age, doing work that only gardeners do in India. Amazing!

Giving Prasad a friendly wave, Ethan turns off the mower. Then, mopping his face with a handkerchief, he walks over. Ethan looks tired, but he is smiling and seems happy to see Prasad, as if this is an agreeable break from a taxing chore. A baseball hat with an unfamiliar logo partly conceals his snowy white hair, and he's wearing a pale blue T-shirt that bears the name of a charity walk. Seeing the wrinkles on his face, Prasad wonders if Ethan is older than him.

"Hello, Mr. Cooper. How are you? You're working hard."

Ethan laughs. "I'm fine. I was wondering about you, though. Yesterday was not a good day. Awfully sorry that you had to experience such abuse. Hope you're okay now."

"I . . . I'm fine," Prasad says, flustered. It didn't occur to him that Ethan had heard the motorist shout at Prasad as he was crossing the street. That explains why he'd pulled over, even before he recognized Prasad. But Ethan hadn't said anything about the motorist then, probably because Prasad was shaken and Ethan didn't want to upset him further. It's only now that Prasad sees how Ethan would have been close enough to hear the motorist yell, "Are you fucking crazy? Go back to your country!"

That's all. Then he was gone, the flashy car roaring as it accelerated. Struck by the man's vehemence, Prasad froze, though only for a moment. Pulling himself together, he slowly continued walking—only to stop when he saw Ethan pull over in his SUV.

"It was my mistake," Prasad says now, facing Ethan as they stand at the edge of Vijay's property. "You see, I was looking in the wrong direction. I don't know why. Although I'm used to left-side driving in my country, I know the traffic rules here."

"Mistakes happen, so there's no need for such rudeness, such abuse," Ethan says, shaking his head. "Motorists have to be careful when they see pedestrians. I don't know what this country is coming to!"

"It's no better back home, Mr. Cooper. In fact, motorists can be worse. I haven't properly thanked you for the lift—"

"Please . . . there's no need. It was my pleasure. I'm glad I happened to be there. Do call me Ethan. What's your name again? Sorry, I'm bad with names."

"Prasad. Looks like you stay pretty active, Mr. . . . I mean, Ethan."

"Well, I try, Prasad." He chuckles. "Did you come alone from India?"

"Yes, I did." Prasad, whose wife died a couple of years ago, doesn't elaborate; he has heard from Vijay that Ethan is a widower as well.

They chat for a few more minutes, mostly about their grandchildren, before Ethan asks if he'd like to join him in the house for a drink.

"I'm not used to alcohol," Prasad says, showing hesitation.

Ethan laughs. "I meant apple cider, Prasad. Or lemonade. Your choice."

After locking the front door with the key Vijay had given him, Prasad enters Ethan's house and follows him to his living room, comfortably furnished with a cushiony sofa set, an easy chair with a lamp beside it, a bright rug, and an oval coffee table covered with books and papers. The blinds of the bay window are open, giving Prasad a view of the sun-dappled backyard and a birdhouse dangling close to the glass. An upright piano is in one corner. A computer on a carved desk is in another corner, which probably means the room doubles as a study. What strikes Prasad the most are the wooden shelves on both sides of a black stereo system. They're filled with rows and rows of CDs and vinyl records.

"That's quite a collection, Ethan," he says. "You must be an aficionado. What sort of music do you like?"

"I'm open to different genres, but these days I tend to listen to classical music. Please have a seat, Prasad. I'll be right back with the lemonade."

They touch on various topics—weather, children, health, travel—before circling back to their interests. Prasad mentions that he used to sketch a lot and even contribute satirical cartoons to a magazine in India. But now he has no such hobby, he admits.

"Personally, I think it's important to continue doing what we enjoy," Ethan says. "I'm guilty of neglecting my own advice. But while I've given up carpentry, which I loved, my interest in music hasn't abated. I'm more of a listener these days."

After confessing that he knows little about Western classical music, Prasad asks if he could listen to something. Ethan, noting that a few CDs have already been loaded in the player, picks up the remote control and presses it. As the lush first movement of Beethoven's Sixth Symphony ("Pastoral") fills the room, he silently hands Prasad a boxed CD set and returns to his chair. The opening melody unfolds at a leisurely pace and the piece has a soothing, elemental beauty, even as it gradually builds in intensity with thrilling variation and repetition. Is it painting musical pictures of pastoral life? Flipping through the CD booklet as he listens, Prasad is startled to see that the symphony's five movements have titles. "Awakening of cheerful feelings on arrival in the countryside," reads the first one, aptly summarizing the mood it evokes.

Prasad gives himself up to the music. The next two movements are called "Scene by the brook" and "Merry gathering of country folk." Ethan seems to have chosen the right piece for a novice, given how effortlessly this bubbling, delightfully meandering symphony, with riffs that mimic bird calls, transports Prasad back to a youthful jaunt by a serenely flowing river in rural India. The flute, so recognizable, is imitating a nightingale, he learns. On that long-ago picnic, overcoming his shyness, he'd spoken to an attractive girl from another group—only to be teased by his friends. Floating in the music's inexorable current, Prasad knows that the descriptions are not meant to be taken literally. But he can't help himself.

The previous day, after signing the form his banker had asked him to send, Prasad set out on his regular walk in the neighborhood. But this time, instead of taking the same route back to the house, he planned to walk past the mailbox he'd seen from his son's car. After mailing his envelope,

Prasad would return to the intersection where his granddaughter's school bus stopped. Uma usually picked her up from school. However, since an office meeting would delay her this afternoon, Vijay had asked Prasad to meet Mala at the bus stop.

Prasad missed the mailbox, unexpectedly. As he recalled, it was in a little plaza near the intersection where Vijay often turned right onto an avenue. But the plaza wasn't in sight, and rather than being close to the avenue, he seemed to be deeper in a maze of residential streets with unrecognizable names. He must have made a wrong turn somewhere. Now he understood the wisdom of owning a smartphone, which he'd been resisting for a long time; even his son seemed a little embarrassed to see him using the outdated flip phone. Prasad, though, could be obstinate. Trying not to panic, he focused on retracing his steps.

It didn't work, and Prasad realized that he was lost. How did that happen when he hadn't walked very far from the house? This area wasn't easy to navigate, apparently, if you were a newcomer and a pedestrian. What his friend had said about the suburbs—"if you don't have a car, you're stuck and out of luck"—was true. Prasad had smiled then, but he didn't feel like smiling now. Determinedly, he turned in what he thought was the right direction and kept walking, quickening his pace and looking around to see if he could speak to anybody. But there was nobody—and the imposing houses he saw, with their tidy yards, were silent and ghostly, as if their owners had abandoned them. It was eerie.

Where were all the people, Prasad had wondered on his first morning in the U.S., as he stood in his son's front yard and looked down the leafy, orderly suburban street? At work, he'd surmised, or behind closed doors in their lovely homes. Cars had gone by every now and then, although he barely caught a glimpse of the passengers. Yes, he did see walkers and joggers later that day. A few had smiled or waved at him, while the others—looking purposeful, as if they had to get somewhere on time—were absorbed in the sounds emanating from their headphones.

What a contrast it was to the way he lived in India, where the hustle and bustle outside his building never seemed to cease, and one couldn't avoid people. Sometimes, it's true, the bazaar-like atmosphere was a little too much, too chaotic. But Prasad was grateful to be in a building where he knew everybody. With his wife gone and his only child living abroad, some of the long-time residents were like family to him. They looked out for him.

Loneliness, he'd heard, was common in highly individualistic societies like America. Yet, despite living in a country that wasn't very individualistic, he'd also experienced loneliness.

A car, turning at the corner, moved in his direction. Eager though he was to ask for help, Prasad hesitated to raise his hand. It felt awkward—what if the driver didn't stop? And then, when the car passed him, it was too late. However, as luck would have it, when he turned at the same corner, the avenue came into view. While this was a different intersection, it looked familiar and he knew that if he crossed to the other side, there was a petrol station. Or, as they liked to say here, a gas station. It had puzzled him at first, until Vijay, who often filled up at this station, told him that gas was short for gasoline.

Crossing the avenue in a hurry, Prasad neglected to look in the proper direction.

After the motorist who yelled at him took off in his car, Prasad—who was walking again—became wary when another vehicle pulled over and the driver, rolling his window down, asked if he needed a ride. But his apprehension turned to relief when he saw Ethan Cooper, Vijay's neighbor. On a couple of occasions, they'd exchanged quick hellos. Ethan recognized him as well, and when Prasad stated that he was trying to reach the bus stop to meet his granddaughter, he merely said, "Hop in."

The ride was short, giving them barely enough time for some casual remarks. Alas, the school bus had already left—again. Saying that Mala would be at her friend's house by now, Prasad asked Ethan to drop him near his son's front door.

Uma, when she came home after picking up her daughter, acted graciously. But Prasad could tell that she was a little annoyed, for she scarcely paid attention to his explanation. He forgot again, she seemed to think. No need for excuses.

Later that night, Prasad stumbled upon a conversation that his son and daughter-in-law were having in the living room, where the TV was on at a low volume and the lights were dimmed. They must have thought he was sleeping. But he hadn't been able to fall asleep, although his light was switched off and he lay comfortably in bed. Feeling thirsty, Prasad got out of bed and left his room—only to stop when he heard their voices. Afraid to announce his presence, he leaned against the wall.

"I'm not making a big deal, Vijay. But how do you expect a young girl to

know whether her grandfather is home? That's why it's better for Mala to go to Amy's place when I can't pick her up. And I don't understand why the suitcase was near the door. I almost stumbled—"

"Papa was looking for some bank documents. He just forgot, Uma. We'll be lucky if we're not forgetful when we reach his age. Think of your dad—"

"Come on, Vijay, this is not about my dad . . . and you know that!"

Soundlessly, Prasad withdrew into his room and got back into bed. As he pulled the blanket close to him, the silence and darkness around him felt like additional layers of protection. The glowing digits of the clock next to his bed said 11:23—which meant that it would be close to 10 in the morning back home. The building would be buzzing with activity, even though a bunch of residents would have left for work or school by now. Homemakers would be busy, while retirees like him would be puttering around in their flats or outside. Prasad imagined being on his little balcony, gazing down on a street that reminded him of a procession during festival time.

One evening, after dinner at Vijay's home, Uma had mentioned that Ethan's daughter came to see him on weekends. And sometimes Ethan visited his daughter and her kids. This bit of information, shared during Prasad's first week in the U.S., had surprised him. Since Ethan's daughter's lived in the same city, why hadn't he—after his wife's death—downsized and moved in with her? Why did he choose to live alone? Was it because people here, as Prasad had once heard a commentator say, were more I-centric than we-centric?

But now, as he was about to drift off to sleep in Vijay's house, Prasad could see Ethan's point. Despite the solitude, perhaps it was better to live on your own as long as you could.

Shortly after listening to the symphony in Ethan's living room, Prasad walks back to his son's house. And that afternoon, before it's time for Uma to return home with her daughter, he heads to Ethan's house again, holding a manila envelope. In it are two Indian classical music CDs that he hopes Ethan will get a chance to sample, given that he'd expressed some curiosity. The lawn mower is in the same spot, as if the job was abandoned halfway.

When Prasad presses the doorbell, there is no response—and he hesitates to press it more than twice. Not having heard the chimes outside, he wonders if the doorbell is out of order. Maybe he should give the envelope to him later, when he is home, rather than leave it on the doorstep. But Ethan's SUV is in the driveway, so he couldn't have gone anywhere.

On a whim, Prasad decides to go to the back of Ethan's property and return to Vijay's house that way. Catching sight of the bay windows, he is reminded of the symphony, especially the last two movements. They were listening to it just a few hours ago. "Storm" and "Shepherd's song"—that's what they're called, aren't they? In the penultimate movement, the rousing music builds to a climax with spectacular sound effects that mimic the foreboding rumble of thunder. Almost involuntarily, as he hears the vigorous beating of drums in his head, Prasad approaches the dangling birdhouse, his attention drawn by a pool of light in the living room.

Ethan might think he is spying on him, but Prasad doesn't care. Is he okay? He looked weary that morning, probably because he'd been mowing. Prasad peers inside. Ethan, at first glance, appears to be reading in his easy chair. But he is not. Slouching forward, with his eyes closed, he seems to be drifting in a tranquil river of dreams, while the lyrical but imagined music of the symphony's finale—the calm after the storm—gently washes over Prasad. An open book is lying on Ethan's lap. What if he is not sleeping?

His pulse racing, Prasad bangs on the glass window. To his relief, Ethan looks up with a start, turns his head towards Prasad—and smiles.

SCHISMS AND SURPRISES

FRAGMENTS OF GLASS

That letter for Suresh, his first one from India in a long time, arrived unexpectedly. The pale blue aerogram with its bright stamps stood out instantly in the little pile of bills, fliers and credit card solicitations he'd retrieved from his mailbox. He looked at in wonder for a few moments. It was from his maternal uncle, Ravi, whom Suresh hadn't seen in two decades. Standing in the lobby of his apartment building, he opened the letter and read it quickly. After some pleasantries and family updates, Ravi wrote that he'd be visiting the U.S. to attend a conference. He included the details of his itinerary. Suresh's uncle lived with his wife and children in a remote town, where he taught sociology at the local university.

To Suresh and his cousins, when they were growing up in India, Ravi, the youngest among his siblings, had seemed like a rebel. With his pensive good looks and unconventional manner, he'd been different from the rest of their traditional, straitlaced family. He usually wore cotton T-shirts or kurtas, and his dark unruly hair, which almost touched his shoulders, invariably attracted disapproving looks from a few elders. It was rumored that he had a girlfriend in the city. During the summer or winter vacation, when Suresh went to his ancestral village, his uncle also made a short visit. Ravi would lounge in his room, listening to music while reading and writing, or he would wander around the paddy fields, an unfiltered Charminar cigarette dangling from his lips. Sometimes he would join the boys for a game of cricket.

Suresh clearly remembered his uncle's last visit to the village, not long before Ravi got engaged to the woman he'd met in college. That day, in the spacious yard of his grandparents' house, Suresh was playing cricket with Bhavani's son, Jagan, who did errands for the household and also took care of the cows. It was hot and muggy as they played, and their faces glistened with sweat in the torpid silence of that long afternoon. Fortunately, every now and then, a strong gust of salty breeze from the sea close by brought some relief.

Behind the house, the drooping coconut trees came to life and, for fleeting moments, swayed like graceful dancers on a stage. Suresh's grandparents were taking their customary daytime nap.

Jagan and his mother lived on the sprawling property in a shed-like building that had a sloping red-tiled roof. Suresh knew that it was his grandfather who supported them. Bhavani's husband, who'd started working for Suresh's grandparents as a boy, had died in a road accident years ago.

Holding his bat in a defensive position, Suresh stood expectantly in the shade of a sweet-smelling jackfruit tree, whose sturdy and capacious trunk acted as the wickets. When only the two of them were playing, Jagan was usually the bowler-cum-fielder. The red ball came flying towards him and Suresh hit it hard, relishing the popping sound of the willow. While he waited for Jagan to fetch the ball, Suresh was startled to see his uncle watching them intently, with a smile on his face and a cigarette hanging from his lips, as he ambled up the path that led to the yard. He had walked from the bus stop close by, carrying his suitcase and bag. With a whoop, Suresh dropped the bat and rushed forward to greet his uncle, and Jagan came from behind to help with the baggage.

Putting his arm around Suresh's shoulders, Ravi said, "That was good batting. I was watching you. Did Jagan also get a chance?"

"He doesn't mind bowling, Ravi Uncle."

"But did you ask him, Suresh?"

"No," he said, feeling guilty. "I'll ask him next time."

Later that evening, when Ravi impulsively asked Jagan to join them for dinner at the small table, there was a shocked silence. Grandma, who was getting ready to serve the food, glared at Ravi but did not speak right away. Dreading an awkward scene, Suresh kept looking at the plate in front of him. Surely, his uncle knew that Jagan never sat at the table with them. He belonged to a low caste. Jagan used his own plate and glass, which were kept on a kitchen shelf, and he always sat on the floor when he ate. Usually, he had dinner with his mother.

"That's okay, Ravi," Grandma finally said. "Jagan will eat later."

But Ravi was not so easily dissuaded. "What's the harm, Amma?" he said. "There's enough room for everyone. Let him join us."

"If that's what you want, I'm leaving." She sounded angry. "You can serve yourselves."

"I can't believe you still do this . . . even after what happened. Let him sit here, Amma."

Without answering, she put the bowl down roughly and left the room, and Suresh realized that she was going to Grandpa's room to check on him. After his stroke, from which he'd only partially recovered, Grandpa was a shadow of his former self. In the past, he'd been distant, irascible, controlling; in a twist of fate, now he was a docile, helpless man who was wholly dependent on his wife.

After what seemed like an interminable pause, Ravi said, "Sit, Jagan." He'd spoken calmly, but there was a look of grim determination on his face. Jagan, looking terrified, obeyed instantly. For the first time in his life, Suresh hated his uncle. He'd made everybody uncomfortable by suddenly changing the rules in the house. Ravi picked up the bowl Grandma had been holding and served the rice. Jagan's usual plate and glass still lay on the kitchen shelf. But Jagan didn't eat with them.

"I have to go," he said abruptly, standing up. His voice quavered and he seemed close to tears. Before Ravi could say anything, Jagan left the room and slipped out of the house. Suresh lost his appetite and he also wanted to get up and walk away. But he couldn't bring himself to defy his uncle.

The following morning, when Jagan was feeding the cows behind the house, Suresh walked over to watch him. Something had been bothering him and he hoped Jagan would shed light on it. One of the cows mooed, perhaps in annoyance, and Suresh retreated to a safe distance.

"Is it true that Grandpa used to come to your house before he got sick?" he asked.

Concentrating on his task, Jagan was slow to respond. "Yes," he finally said, looking up.

"Why?" He'd heard whispered rumors, and now as he waited for a direct answer from Jagan, Suresh could feel his heart thumping vigorously.

This time Jagan did not look at him. "To see my mother," he said softly.

A few days later, when Ravi received a long-awaited job offer, he hastily packed all his things and left for the university. At the end of that summer, Suresh told his parents he didn't want to spend any more vacations with his grandparents. Surprisingly they didn't ask for a reason, and from then on Suresh went to the village only for very short visits. He seldom saw Jagan, who had now begun to work longer hours in the fields, and even when they did meet on that rare occasion, their interaction was a little awkward and perfunctory. There were no more cricket games. Suresh's grandparents died when he was in high school, and he lost touch with Jagan.

At the airport, having arrived early, Suresh became nervous about meeting his uncle after all these years. Would it be tentative at first? What was he going to say to him?

Suresh wasn't sure if he would recognize him, but he needn't have worried. Although Ravi was nearly bald and had gained weight, his face hadn't aged much and he was instantly recognizable. He greeted Suresh effusively and before long they were chatting with easy familiarity; it was as if they'd stayed in touch all along. After stopping for dinner at a Mexican restaurant, they drove to Suresh's apartment building. Ravi was going to spend the night with him, and after meeting his friend at a local university the following day, he planned to leave for the conference in another city.

"Suresh, I thought you'd be married by now," Ravi said, entering the building.

"You sound like my mother now, Uncle."

Ravi chuckled. "You know, Jagan is married to a nice girl. They have a child."

When Suresh heard that name, a buried emotion bubbled to the surface. He fumbled with his keys. Suresh often felt guilty that he'd cut Jagan off so completely. Even before he left for the U.S., Suresh hadn't tried to contact him to say goodbye.

"How is Jagan?" he asked. "Where is he these days?"

"In his village. They all live in Grandpa's house, which he now owns. Didn't you know that?"

Stunned by the news, Suresh couldn't speak for a moment. "No," he said at last. The food they had eaten made him thirsty and his mouth felt dry. He asked his uncle if he wanted a drink. When Ravi shook his head and flopped on the sofa, Suresh walked to the kitchenette. They were silent for a few moments. Suresh wanted to ask his uncle something, but he hesitated.

"I suppose you also don't know why I'm estranged from the family," Ravi said, as if he'd read Suresh's mind.

"No, Uncle, I don't. Nobody told me anything."

"It doesn't surprise me." Ravi laughed bitterly. "You know, Suresh, we certainly know how to keep secrets in our family. I was accused of coercing Grandpa to give the house and a portion of the land to Jagan and his mother.

It's not true, although I did make that suggestion before relinquishing my claim. I think the old man made the right decision. After all, Jagan was his child."

The glass Suresh was holding, and filling with chilled water from the refrigerator, slipped from his hand and crashed on the shiny floor. Instead of looking at his uncle, who had risen from the sofa, Suresh stared in shock at the glittering fragments of glass that lay scattered in the expanding pool of water.

A year later, almost to the week, Suresh traveled by bus to his ancestral village in India. He'd finally managed to take time off from work for a vacation, and this was his last stop on the itinerary. Months earlier, upon hearing that Jagan's mother had died, Suresh managed to track down his phone number in the village. On a static-filled line that cut them off a couple of times, they spoke amiably. Sounding very pleased to hear from him, Jagan cordially invited him for a visit on his next trip to India.

What had been a sleepy village was now a bustling little town, a place that seemed relatively prosperous but also more crowded and dirtier. As Suresh emerged from the bus station, which looked newly built, a lanky man approached him from a teashop nearby. Suresh recognized Jagan right away. His boyish features and that quick smile, which lit up his big dark eyes, were so familiar to him.

Suresh noticed many changes around him, but the ancestral house looked much the same from a distance. Up close, though, it looked out of date compared to the other houses that had sprung up in the neighborhood, and he could see that it needed some repairs and a fresh coat of paint. As Suresh walked across the neatly maintained yard, which seemed less spacious than before, pleasant memories of his childhood came flooding back.

Much of the old furniture was still there, and judging by the absence of any updating either inside or outside the house, Suresh realized that Jagan hadn't prospered that much—at least, not yet. With her daughter in tow, Jagan's wife entered the room and shyly greeted Suresh. After some coaxing, the girl came closer and accepted his gift. Then, despite Suresh's protests, Jagan's wife returned to the kitchen to continue preparing an elaborate meal in his honor.

"It's good to see you here again, Jagan, after all these years," Suresh said, sitting down. "I wish I had come earlier to see your mother."

"Yes, she would have loved that. She had fond memories of you."

Jagan asked him to stay for a few days, but Suresh regretfully said that he had to leave the next day because of his tight schedule. Although their conversation was wide-ranging, they tactfully avoided any awkward discussion of their past. Looking at Jagan, as he sat on a chair and casually talked about his family, Suresh realized that their childhood days in the village truly belonged to another—and thankfully distant—era. He could see that Jagan was completely at home in this ancient house.

When Jagan went to the kitchen to get some water, Suresh walked up to the back window. His eyes instinctively searched for the outbuilding on the property. He did not see it.

"It's not there," Jagan said quietly. "I tore it down."

Startled by his sudden appearance, Suresh turned and saw him standing close by, a glass of cold water in his hand. Jagan's manner was friendly and gentle, as always, but now Suresh could detect sadness in his voice. There was no hint of bitterness.

"Yes, I'm glad it's no longer there, Jagan," he said, taking the glass from him. Then, holding it firmly, Suresh drank the refreshing water slowly and gratefully.

RIVER OF SILENCE

Leaning forward from the edge of the terrace, with her heels raised and right arm outstretched, she saw them first—and knew, even before they stopped and looked up, that they weren't passing by. They were coming to the house. One was a man—sturdy and dark, with thick hair that was fully white—and he had a pained expression, as if he were watching the beginning of a disastrous stunt. But the boy next to him was grinning. Taller than the man, with curly black hair and a slender body, he was wearing tight pants and a light brown T-shirt with writing on it. Meena couldn't read the words, but she could see the dark pools of his eyes as he gazed up at her. He crossed the road, without looking away, and the man followed him.

It wasn't a big house despite the two stories, and the boy didn't look concerned. The man, though, was alarmed. Yes, there was a gap in the terrace wall, but did he really think she wouldn't be careful, that she would slip and plummet to the ground? If she came across as an acrobat or a diva, poised for a spectacular climax, he was like an agitated fan. Vigorously waving his arms, he shouted warnings, prompting Meena to step back and return to her chair. It was only a few yards away, in a safe corner, over which the drooping, full-leaved branches of a jackfruit tree formed an agreeable canopy. It was her favorite spot. She picked up her book, just as the man and the boy, who seemed to be about her age, walked up to the front door.

Later, when Meena thought about her stay in the village, she realized how uneventful it would have been if these two visitors hadn't shown up that day. Bored by the place, after the novelty quickly wore off, she was spending a lot of time reading, desperately waiting to leave.

The doorbell rang, and she heard voices. Opening her book, she settled back in the wicker chair. Meena decided to give her dad and great-aunt a chance to speak with the guests, but at some point she'd have to go down and meet them. Over dinner the previous evening, her dad had mentioned that his childhood friend would be coming to see him.

That's when her great-aunt, while serving them prawn curry, had said, "He's come a long way. He's made something of himself, overcoming disadvantages. Remember how poor his family was back then? They used to live in a hut. He had to work from an early age. I still have that picture . . . of you, him and the other boy you played with."

"Yes, I saw it, along with the other pictures on the wall," Meena's dad said.

"Those two boys belonged to the same community and the families were struggling, but their lives took such different turns. I don't know if you told Meena—"

"Isn't his son coming as well?" he asked. Meena sensed the impatience in her dad's voice—he was more interested in the present than the past. But was he also trying to avoid talking about something painful?

"I believe so," her great-aunt said. "His name is Kishore. A nice boy, though I don't know him well. He is maybe a couple of years older than Meena. Things are different here now. People mingle more easily . . . there's more confidence, less distance. It's not like the old days."

"Yes, but how deep is the change, really?" Meena's dad said. She saw a flash of irritation in his eyes, and there was a tremor of exasperation in his voice.

But her great-aunt was not deterred. Unlike back then, she noted with pride, Kishore's father now sat in her living room and ate at her table. There wasn't a separate plate or glass for him, as the local custom had dictated in the old days. He was like any other guest, she claimed. So what if he'd had a menial job in the household as a youngster? That was history. There was wonder in her voice, as she reflected on the changes she'd seen in her village over a long life—but there was also, Meena couldn't help thinking, more than a touch of defensiveness.

Somebody knocked loudly on the front door. Rising, Meena's great-aunt said the man who was going to bring fresh fish the next morning had come to collect money. When she returned to the table, dinner was almost over and the conversation drifted to other matters.

Meena resumed reading, though she kept thinking about the guests, especially the boy, who had continued to look up, still smiling, even when he couldn't see her. Thankfully, her stay in the ancestral village was coming to an end. She was eager to get on the plane. Honestly, she couldn't understand how her urbane dad—who was so city-centric back home that her mom had to use her considerable persuasive powers to make him move to the suburbs—felt at home in this rustic environment. Sure, it was picturesque, surrounded as they were by lush green paddy fields dotted with coconut and palm trees—while in the hazy distance, she could catch the glimmer of the brackish sea. But the sandy stretch that passed for a beach wasn't inviting. Although she'd enjoyed looking at the endless sheet of shimmering blue water when she went there, what stood out for her was the overpowering smell of fish. Several fisherwomen had laid them out to dry that morning. As for the chattering fishermen, Meena could see some of them in their bobbing boats, where they were attending to their nets in preparation for the next expedition.

Sometimes, looking around, Meena felt she was on a tropical film set. Her dad was playing an unfamiliar role, a role that had more to do with his childhood. And what about her? Was she also playing a role, learning her lines and deciphering the story as she went along?

There was also a river here, she'd heard, not far from the house. It wasn't visible from where she was sitting, but she could see the hill that blocked it from view. When she asked her dad, he downplayed its importance and said it wasn't worth going there. It was a tributary actually, he added, though it's true that back when he was a child, it had felt like a river because of the volume of water. Now it was a sluggish, muddy stream.

"What are you reading?"

A startled Meena, raising her head, saw the boy standing fairly close to her. A breeze from the sea played with his curly hair, strands of which touched his eyebrows. He seemed like another actor in the film unspooling in her mind—and though his role remained unclear to her, he had no trouble with his lines. He exuded confidence and charm. For a moment, as she wondered how he'd appeared on the terrace so quietly, they heard the tinkling of bells. A cowherd was passing by, taking the cattle home after a grazing session near the hill.

The boy had spoken in the local language—which Meena knew, though not fluently.

"I'm reading a storybook," she said. It sounded unserious, but she didn't know the right word. So she added, in English, "It's a novel."

"Okay." He smiled. Then, switching to the local language, he said, "Do you read a lot of books in America? Your great-aunt says that you love to read."

Closing her book, Meena rose from her chair. "I don't know if it's a lot. There's not much to do here—so I read. Are you a student?"

"No, I'm not. I work."

She felt her face flush. Changing the subject, Meena said that she liked the quote (she used the English word) on his T-shirt. "Don't Count the Days," it read.

"It's not complete," he said. "Can you guess what it says on the back?"

"'Make the Days Count'? I expected the entire quote to be on the front, but I think this way is better. Wasn't it Muhammad Ali who said it?"

"Yes, you're right! I call this my American or Ali T-shirt."

Saying that she should get her own Ali T-shirt, Meena asked if she was wanted downstairs. No, Kishore said, adding that his father and her dad were having a good chat, not having seen each other in a while. He'd come up to meet her. Unlike his father, who had been worried that she might fall, he knew she wasn't in danger and was reaching for a guava.

"Are there guavas in America?" he asked. "Do you like them a lot?"

Meena was, again, struck by his boldness. He wasn't like the other boys she'd seen here, boys who shrank from her—but were, at the same time, fascinated as they observed her from a distance, only to turn away quickly when she glanced at them. This happened whenever she went out, either with her dad or great-aunt, to shop, meet people they knew, or do some sightseeing in the area. But there wasn't much to do in this rural backwater, pretty though it was, and she mostly stayed home, making the terrace her retreat. It was winter, thank goodness, allowing her to enjoy the balmy weather and the gentle breeze that rustled the leaves above her. Summer here would be oppressive, unbearable.

Her dad, she was sure, would be at ease here even in the summer. Far from being bored, he was having a good time and seemed, at least to her, like a local—although he'd lived in the village only for a few months as a child when his parents were doing research on a remote island. When they returned, he joined them in the city, where he mostly grew up and studied before moving abroad as a young man for an advanced degree.

Once, after checking with her dad, who was tied up with some paperwork, Meena walked alone to the colorful bazaar. She got the same curious glances and smiles, but she didn't speak to anybody or buy anything.

When her great-aunt heard about it, her expression showed disapproval, as if she'd bitten an unripe guava—and though she didn't say anything, it was clear she wasn't happy about Meena taking such solitary trips.

"Yes, they grow in some places," Meena said. "I like guavas when they're soft and sweet."

"Who doesn't?" Kishore laughed. "My father mentioned how he and your father and another boy used to pluck guavas from the trees without telling anybody. Then they'd head to the hill there to eat them. I wonder if they're talking about the river now."

"The river? I don't understand. Why would they be talking about the river?"

"There was an incident," he said, his eyes widening. "I thought you'd know about it. Never mind . . . it happened a long time ago."

"I didn't hear about it," she said. "He might have told my mother, but I have no idea. Can you tell me now?"

Kishore smiled uncertainly, as if in regret. And she saw that he was torn, eager but also afraid to say more. "I don't know . . . I'm not sure about the details," he finally said. "Maybe you should ask your father."

"Why?" she said, her eyebrows arching. "You seem to know what happened. Why aren't you saying anything?" Coming closer, she stared at him and added, mischievously, "Do you want to hide it from me?"

"No, of course not!" Her remark stung, she could tell. "It's just that . . . well, it happened so long ago—"

"Why don't we go to the river now?"

"What?" he said, taken aback. "What for? It's not much to look at these days."

"It doesn't matter," she said. "I won't be here for long, and I haven't seen it. Let's go. It's not far."

When Meena later looked back on this moment, she couldn't say why he suddenly agreed—and she couldn't explain why she had this crazy impulse to go there without informing anybody. Urging Kishore to follow her, she went down the stairs and slipped through the side gate to the lane outside. Nobody inside the house had seen her.

She saw Kishore pause on the stairs, as if he were trying to convince himself that her decision to go to the river wasn't reckless—before he came down and joined her. They walked quietly, their arms touching, until they reached the bend and could no longer see the house. A few people glanced at them, but the direction in which they were walking, away from the market center, was sparsely populated and they didn't attract much attention. It didn't take long to reach the hill, which had brown patches but was mostly green with thick vegetation in the middle.

"Is everybody rich in America?" he asked, as they began the ascent.

"What?" She laughed, surprised as much by the question as its timing. "Far from it. Where do you get your news from? I think there are false . . . how should I say it?" Struggling to translate 'misconceptions,' she added, "I think people here have false views of life there."

"Yes, just as people there have false views of life here." He grinned.

"You're so right," she said, holding his arm for support.

They stopped when the river became visible. Meena withdrew her arm. The river was depleted and tame—but looking at the hollowed out earth, she could tell that, decades ago, the water here had flowed swiftly, forcefully. Now the level was so low that one could walk in the riverbed. Silently, it twisted away from them towards the sea.

Kishore clasped her hand—but almost immediately, as if he'd received a jolt of electricity, he released it. The movie in her head was taking an unexpected turn. She still didn't know his role. Turning her head, she saw that his face had turned red. He was staring ahead, anxiously, but when she smiled, his face brightened. He held her hand again, a little awkwardly.

"Do you want to go down to the river?" he said. "Or should we go back?"

"There's not much to see here, as you said. So, did my father fall into the river?"

Kishore looked stunned. "You already know, don't you? You know what happened."

"I guessed," she said in English, shrugging. As before, when the word she needed in the local language eluded her, she spoke in English. He understood her, in any case. Chuckling, she continued, "Maybe I read too many novels. But you can tell me what happened. I could be wrong, of course."

"No, you're not. He did fall into the river. Your father couldn't swim—at least, back then. So my father rescued him when he fell from the canoe they were in."

Meena stood gazing at him, without speaking, and hoped he'd continue with the story. But Kishore had nothing more to say about it. Instead, he said, "Let's go back. It's going to get dark soon. They'll be wondering about us."

"Fine," she said, turning around. They'd already disengaged their hands, but as Meena started walking down the slope, she stumbled. He caught her by the arm just in time. When he gently pulled her up and towards him, she became tense. His lips were parted and he was looking down at her mouth. Was he going to kiss her? Meeting his gaze, she shivered. But she wasn't alarmed. The nervousness she felt was reflected in his eyes. He tightened his grip—and then froze, perhaps out of fear. He released her. Meena relaxed, as did he, though her relief was tinged with sadness.

Acting more businesslike now, they resumed walking and reached the bottom much faster than they'd gone up. They were intent on getting back to the house. The daylight was leaking out of the sky, leaving lengthening shadows on the ground—and the birds, silent till now, were chirping in chorus. The approaching night seemed like a slowly descending curtain. Abruptly, the screen in Meena's head went dark, and though she couldn't tell if the movie had come to an end, she did feel less detached from her surroundings.

The house loomed into view, and they increased their pace.

"I think that's your father," Meena said.

Indeed, it was, although they couldn't see his face. Walking past the house, he was going in the other direction. Had he come towards the hill, initially, before deciding to turn around?

"He's looking for us," Kishore said. "But don't worry . . . I'll talk to him."

Sprinting forward, Kishore caught up with him—and as Meena approached the house, she could see them talking rapidly. Kishore's father seemed angry and he was gesticulating wildly, his face still turned away from her. Should she walk up to them? Then, as she watched in astonishment, he slapped Kishore—and, following the briefest of pauses, struck him again. She could scarcely believe it. Shocked, she stood still.

"Meena, go inside!"

It was her great-aunt. Standing on the terrace, with her arms crossed, she was staring grimly at Meena. Where was her dad? Silently, as her eyes clouded over, Meena opened the side gate and walked into the house.

In her dorm room, taking a break from an assignment for her literature class, Meena was scrolling through the emails in her inbox when two words—

"Kishore's father"— jumped out, transfixing her. Staring at the unusual subject line, she hesitated to go any further. What did her dad have to say about him? Meena was in college now, living away from home for the first time. On their last phone call, earlier in the week, he hadn't said anything about Kishore or his father. In fact, they hadn't talked about them since their trip a few years ago. Taking off her headphones to shut out the music, she clicked open the email and read it slowly.

Dear Meena,

We spoke just two days ago, but late last night, I got some terrible news that I wanted to share with you. Kishore's father died unexpectedly. I don't have all the details, though I know it was a heart attack. I managed to get a plane ticket and I'm waiting at the gate to board. I'll call you after I get there, but I feel compelled to share something now.

You already know that Kishore's father saved me when our canoe capsized in the river. What you don't know is that there was another boy who didn't make it. Yes, he was in that picture you saw at the house. Only Kishore's father could swim, unfortunately. He was filled with guilt and sorrow that he couldn't save the other boy as well. The boy got swept farther down the river, and it was too late to do anything. I often wondered why he'd chosen me, why he didn't try to rescue the other boy first. But he didn't want to talk about it, understandably. And I promised not to say anything about the tragedy while he was still alive. I don't think even Kishore knows what exactly happened that awful day.

I'm writing to you now because I cannot keep this secret any longer, and I want you to think well of him. I know you were distressed when he hit Kishore. You thought he was callous and narrow-minded, even though I assured you that he wasn't. The river—or rather, the incident of that dark day—was the reason he got so upset. Although the river is very different now, the memory of it was still so painful that he got agitated when Kishore said the two of you had gone there. He was afraid, you see. Anyway, that's what I believe. I hope this will help you understand him better. Maybe I could have waited to tell you in person, but I wanted to get it off my chest.

Kishore is doing well, by the way. Perhaps you can talk to him and offer your condolences. I'll give you a call when I see him. He got married last year, I heard. Take care.

Love,
Dad

Meena got the call as she was heading for lunch in the college cafeteria. The morning's last class had just ended, and the promise of a leisurely lunch after being cooped up in a chilly room had loosened tongues around her. But the hubbub was so loud that Meena wouldn't have heard the phone if it hadn't been on vibrate. Ducking back into the big room that had emptied out, she shut the door and answered the call. "Sorry, Meena, if it's a bad time. I'm calling because Kishore is here. Can you talk now?"

"Yes, Dad, it's not a problem. My class is over."

"Glad to hear it," he said. Then the line got staticky, and for a moment Meena thought she was going to lose the connection. But after a brief pause she heard Kishore's voice—loud and clear, as if he were in the same room as her.

"Hello, Meena, how are you?" he said in English.

"Fine, Kishore. My deep condolences. I was very sorry to hear about your loss. Your father was a good man. I hope you and your mother are doing okay."

"Yes . . . your father helping." Then, switching to the local language, he added, "I'm glad your father could come so quickly. We're grateful. They were close friends. When are you going to visit us?"

"Next year, maybe. I'll let you know. Congratulations. I heard that you got married."

"Yes, thank you. My wife is expecting. You should stay with us next time, even if it's for a day or two. I'll show you around. We're in a different town now, not far away. But it's still small, and maybe you'll find it boring here."

"No, of course not." She felt her ears burn. "I'm older now . . . " Meena wanted to elaborate, though she didn't know what she was going to say.

It seemed like Kishore also wanted to keep talking, but there were people around him and she could hear other voices close by, sounding a little impatient. He was obviously busy. The call ended, after quick goodbyes, and she was abruptly drawn back to the icy vacant room. The silence was disconcerting. The two friends who had been walking in front of her hadn't come back to look for her, and there were no text messages. Perhaps they assumed she had other plans. Whatever. She should contact them, Meena thought, looking at her phone again. How weird it felt to be sitting here alone, surrounded by empty seats, as if she were waiting for the next class to begin, a class that would have no other students.

MEMORIES OF MISSION VALLEY

The woman who met me at the entrance of Mission Valley School, my alma mater in India, seemed to know me. But I didn't recognize her.

"You were in the American boy's class, weren't you?" she said, even before I introduced myself. "We called him AB."

"Arun Brown?"

She giggled. "Yes. AB stood for American Boy more than Arun Brown, so I couldn't remember his name. He was here not long ago, visiting from America."

"Really? I'm sorry I missed him."

Earlier that morning, after checking out of my hotel in the district capital, where I'd attended a wedding, I caught a cab that took me along a winding, rising mountain highway, over which hung a gently rolling canopy of mist. When we reached the town, which was crowded and traffic-clogged, the landmarks had changed so much—with new buildings everywhere in a chaotic jumble of concrete—that I got confused and we missed a turn. Then I saw Mission Valley School, perched on a hill. We swung around and went up a narrow road, now fully paved and skirted by eucalyptus and pine trees that had thinned over the years, giving the campus less seclusion. But the heady scent in the crisp air was still the same, beckoning me like a long-lost friend.

The mention of Arun Brown took me back a quarter-century.

It was on the steps of this entrance that I'd first seen him through the bay window of our classroom. Like Arun, I turned sixteen that year. I was thinking about dinner that evening, impatiently waiting for our study hour to end, when I heard an excited announcement in the classroom: "The American boy is here!"

We rushed to the window for a better look. Craning my neck, I saw Ahmed's rickety cab wheezing up the steep driveway, trailing a cloud of red dust in the fading light. In the portico, where the lights had just sprung to life, a sari-clad woman and a tall boy, with curly hair and sporting a navy-blue blazer, emerged from the black-and-yellow Ambassador and walked up the steps, followed by Ahmed, who carried two suitcases.

In the silence that followed, the disappointment in our classroom was palpable. Most of us had expected to see a fair-complexioned, blond-haired, blue-eyed boy. Instead, here was somebody who looked like us! "He is American?" Mohan said, his voice ringing with incredulity. "This must be a different boy."

That's how I felt, but another student who seemed to know better insisted that it was indeed the American boy. The dinner bell rang, shifting our attention to more urgent matters.

Arun Brown wasn't in the dining hall—apparently he and his mother had returned to the hotel for another night—but there was much talk about him. Yes, he had grown up in America. Who was his father? An African-American, apparently, though we said "Negro" back then, unaware—until our dorm master corrected us the following morning—that the word was offensive, not just outdated. Arun's divorced Indian mother had returned to India with Arun and was now teaching at a college. The only Americans I'd seen so far were the white tourists who passed through our town. Like the other students at my table, I could hardly wait to meet Arun the next day.

In my final term at Mission Valley, before our class scattered to tentatively begin our early adulthood in various towns and cities, not to mention junior colleges, Arun breezed into our lives like an unexpected yet welcome guest. It was one of those years that divide your life into before and after. And not just for those of us finishing school. This was 1984, a year that turned out to be tumultuous for India, which had gained independence less than four decades earlier. The troubles in the state of Punjab came to a head that year, with a military assault on Amritsar's Golden Temple to flush out Sikh militants; then there was the assassination of Prime Minister Indira Gandhi, followed by orchestrated massacres of Sikhs by rampaging mobs. Not to forget, there was a horrific industrial disaster of epic proportions in the city of Bhopal.

The Indian state seemed to be unraveling as the year progressed, but at Mission Valley we continued to live in a cocoon, absorbed by our daily routines and petty dramas. When Arun joined our class that morning, it was still early in the year, with a cold snap that would last another two months, and we had little inkling of what lay ahead. It was an English class and we were reading George Orwell's *1984*, curiously enough. Arun walked in with our principal, who interrupted the class and briefly introduced Arun before asking him to sit at the empty desk between Mohan's and mine. If the three of us hadn't been sitting together, I'm sure we wouldn't have become close friends.

Looking back, I realize Arun came to our school probably because the principal didn't mind that, unlike us, Arun wouldn't be taking the all-India board exam at the end of the term. And in fact, he did go back to America to finish high school. The months Arun spent with us might have been a sabbatical of sorts for him, but he fully immersed himself in our academic and extracurricular activities. Well built and taller than almost any other boy, he quickly made friends with his genial, outgoing personality. His American background made him exotic and popular at our school. Some people, especially the kitchen staff and dorm ayahs, simply called him American Boy. Eventually, his nickname became AB.

Mission Valley School, despite the name, wasn't a relic of the Raj. The neo-Gothic brick buildings of our small campus did remind one of a different era, but the British missionaries—for whose children the school had been originally established—had decamped long ago, leaving behind only traces of their colonial education system. I suppose we did live in a kind of Anglo-India, though the emphasis was clearly on India, with the Anglo part influencing our lives mostly in subtle ways. We spoke English frequently, and our library was neatly stocked with books by English authors ranging from Dickens, Austen, Maugham and Greene to perennial favorites like P. G. Wodehouse, Enid Blyton and Arthur Conan Doyle. And yet, more than "bloody hell" and "bugger off," our speech was flavored with colorful Indianisms drawn from a few languages.

Although not familiar with Indian history, Arun became an enthusiastic participant in class, and he made great progress with Hindi, our second language. His popularity soared when he excelled in cricket, which he had never played before. Arun introduced us to baseball, whose rules—like a lot about America, that distant but fascinating country—were mysterious to us. In fact, until Arun's arrival, America had registered in our lives only in the form of movies and comic books, which we avidly consumed and passed around. This was still the pre-globalization era, with no television at our school to bring us news and views from the larger world, and even American pop music—which we sometimes heard, thanks to the boys who had relatives in the U.S.—remained alien to many of us. We could relate better to the sounds of Bollywood films.

Arun became our interpreter of all things American. And it wasn't just students who peppered him with questions. Once in our world history class, we read that Mount Rushmore had sculptures of four leading U.S. presidents who represented the period stretching from the Revolutionary War to the Civil War. Arun then added that a place called Stone Mountain Park featured the carvings of three Civil War leaders who had been heroes in the South but villains in the North. Our history teacher, I remember, was just as intrigued to hear about it. Years later, when I moved to that area, one of the first things I did was to visit Stone Mountain Park and gaze at the rock carvings of those rebel leaders.

There was another side to Arun, I soon realized. But that part of his personality only emerged when he was with Mohan and me.

My favorite time of the day was before study hour. Every weekday, after classes and outdoor activities, we would either bathe or wash up and then have tea and snacks in the dining hall. What followed, before darkness fell and the lights in our school came on, was a delicious stretch of time we called free period. We lounged about, listened to music, read, chatted, and played games like caroms, ping-pong and chess. In those final months, I often hung out with Arun and Mohan. What we enjoyed most was to walk up to Top Point, the highest section of a terraced field where our staff grew vegetables, and sit near a locked shed containing gardening tools. We had a spectacular view of the town.

Students were discouraged from going up to Top Point because of its remoteness, but we went anyway, knowing that nobody else would be around, to enjoy the scenery and smoke a cigarette while chatting. Once Mohan brought a joint, mostly to impress Arun, who smiled and politely took a couple of puffs. Mohan didn't repeat the offer.

The best moment at Top Point—the moment we all waited for before heading down—was when the evening train departed for the plains. Steam engines had already been phased out on the broad-gauge lines, but not here in the Hill District, where an aging narrow-gauge line snaked up to our town. Three toots announced the so-called toy train's departure every evening. As it gathered speed, with the sound echoing in the valley, we would watch the chugging engine belch smoke—which curled lazily before vanishing—and wait by the shed till the train also disappeared from sight. Then we would rush back.

One evening, while we were waiting for the train to leave, Mohan asked casually, "AB, did you have a girlfriend in America?"

"Yes," he said. "I dated some girls, and had a girlfriend."

To my embarrassment, I heard myself say, "So you knew her intimately?"

Arun smiled. "Yes, I knew her intimately, as you put it."

I felt a stab of envy, though I shouldn't have been surprised. It's true that Arun had been circumspect about his relationships with girls. He'd sometimes talked about his American friends, but never girlfriends. And while Mohan and I had privately wondered about his experiences with girls, we hadn't broached the subject because we didn't—or at least I didn't—want to dwell on our inexperience. Being ignorant would be better, I felt, given how often I thought about girls.

The wound festered, making me uncomfortable. Until now I'd only admired Arun and thought it was cool—a word we'd recently picked up—that we could be close friends. But we belonged to different worlds, I suddenly realized. I had never even held hands with a girl.

"Do you have a girlfriend now?" Mohan asked.

Arun smiled and, without saying anything, stubbed out his cigarette. Three sharp toots punctured the silence; it was time for us to get back. We stood up to watch. A muffled *clackety-clack* drifted upwards from the twisting railway tracks, accompanied by plumes of smoke. Soon, the chugging train disappeared under a thick blanket of vegetation, and the reverberations stopped.

"I'm going to get a girlfriend before the term is over," Mohan announced.

I looked at him in shock. "Where are you going to find one?" I asked.

"Well, how about right here in the school?"

Arun and I laughed. "Mohan, what are you talking about?" Arun said.

"There's a girl here that I'm interested in," Mohan said. "And she's interested in me. You may not call her my girlfriend, but I promise I'll kiss her before the term is over."

"Who is she?" I asked. It was hard to believe him, because the school was not co-educational back then. The school began accepting girls a few years after I graduated.

Without answering, Mohan continued walking down the hill. Arun and I followed him.

"He's kidding," Arun whispered to me. "There's no such girl."

Mohan heard him. "Yes, there is!" he said, spinning around. "Let's have a bet."

I looked at him curiously, struck by the emotion in his voice. Arun, too, was looking at him, and he laughed when Mohan said the bet would be worth 100 rupees.

"So, you're going to kiss a girl, right?" Arun said.

"No, not just kiss a girl. It's going to be more than that, AB."

I was dumbfounded. As I stared at Mohan, Arun said, "What do you mean? You can't be serious."

"I am serious," Mohan said calmly. "Intimacy is serious." Then, turning around, he sprinted towards the classroom.

Later in the evening, when we were in the dining hall, it became obvious that Mohan wasn't joking. While some of my tablemates, including Arun, were talking excitedly about an upcoming cricket match, I noticed Mohan exchanging smiles with Swati, who worked in the kitchen along with her mother. Having dropped out of school in her village not long ago, Swati, who didn't speak English, had moved with her mother to our campus, where Sawti's father was our maintenance man. They all lived in a ramshackle building that housed the support staff, whom many people referred to as servants back then.

Mohan's smile had been so fleeting that, at first, I thought I was mistaken. Swati rushed back to the kitchen after depositing a big bowl of steaming rice on one of the tables, and I didn't see her again that evening. But when Mohan grinned at me, I knew it wasn't my imagination. I was flabbergasted. How could he even contemplate doing such a thing?

"Are you serious about your bet?" I whispered.

"Of course," Mohan whispered back, still grinning. "And I'm going to win it soon if everything goes smoothly. Please don't say anything to Arun."

Before we went to bed that night, Mohan sidled up to me in the dorm and took me aside. "It will happen tomorrow evening when everybody is watching the Saturday movie," he said. "Can you bring Arun to the tool shed at eight? Swati is going to meet me there. She has the key."

"This is a bad idea," I said, nervously looking around to see if anybody was watching us. "Does she know what it's about?"

"Kind of . . . I said it was important, that I had something to share with her. Just do it, *yaar*. What's the big deal? She's okay with it."

"It's a big deal, Mohan. I don't think you should do it."

"Fine," he said in a huff. "You don't have to be involved. Be a chicken."

I didn't see Mohan the next day, even in the dorm, and on Sunday I was stunned to hear that he was leaving the school. I never spoke to him again.

"You were in the American boy's class, weren't you?" the woman had said.

Of course, now I remembered her. It was Swati, though I found little resemblance between this amiable woman and the quiet, wispy girl I had known. The matron in charge wouldn't be back till late in the evening, Swati explained, but I was welcome to look around after signing my name in the visitor's book. "It's not a problem; I already know who you are," she added. Again, I was struck by how quickly she'd remembered me.

In the visitor's book, next to his name and address, Arun had included the following comment: "Nice to be back. Brought back memories, good and bad. All the best!" After signing my name, I jotted down Arun's information, promising myself to contact him once I returned to the States.

"We didn't see Mohan again," Swati said. "Do you remember him, the boy who was expelled?"

Startled, I looked up. It was as if she could read my thoughts. There was a grim look on her face, but the moment passed and she was friendly again. What exactly had happened that night, precipitating such a swift expulsion?

"Yes, I remember him," I simply replied, and waited for her to say more. She didn't. I didn't either, as Swati opened another door and let me enter the main campus to visit my boyhood haunts.

ANIL'S VISIT

Facing the building after he stepped out of the cab, Anil experienced—once again—a frisson of surprise. Never having stayed in a place like this, why did the Devi Residency look so familiar? He'd felt the same way, days earlier, when he came across its picture online while doing research for his trip. Sitting at a desk halfway around the world, with his hand on the mouse, he was so struck by the quaint old building that, after reaching for his credit card, he booked a room in the lodging house. Anil had, until now, seen no reason to visit the town where he'd briefly lived as a child—but when he chanced upon the Devi's website, it took him only a moment to make his decision. Finally, after three decades, he'd be back in the town. For what, though? Both his parents were gone, he scarcely remembered what now seemed like a city, and there was just one person still living there who had a connection to the family. Nevertheless, Anil, who unexpectedly got some extra time for his trip, knew he had to go there, if only to stay at the Devi Residency.

"Yes, I've passed it many times," Colonel Mistry wrote, in his response to Anil's email. "Do give me a ring me after you check in. Let's meet. I can see why you picked the Devi. It's comfortable, it has character—but also, isn't there a personal connection?"

Anil took a deep breath. So he wasn't wrong to think the building had a link to his past. Not as a lodging house, of course, because that was only a decade old. What had it been earlier? A private residence, perhaps, although it was hard to believe that his family could have known the owner. Busy with last-minute tasks before his departure, Anil let the thought hang in the air. Just as the swirling mist on his early-morning commute cleared up by the time he reached his office, the question would be answered in due course—or, at least, he hoped so. His online searches had yielded nothing.

In the original plan, Anil's wife and son, who was about to start college, were going to accompany him to India for a short vacation. They'd discussed it as a "return to roots" visit, at least for his wife, who still had relatives in her family's ancestral town. For Anil, an economist, the main purpose of the trip was to present a paper on wage inequality at an academic conference. But then his mother-in-law, who was ailing, needed help when the live-in caretaker quit suddenly. So both Anil's wife and son decided to drop out and spend time with her parents on the East Coast, where Anil's wife had grown up after moving to the U.S. as a child. Anil and his wife had met at a Midwestern university, where he'd enrolled as a foreign graduate student. Starting out as friends, they fell in love and decided to get married after receiving their degrees.

The unanticipated gap in Anil's itinerary gave him another reason for making a stop in this town before his conference. In his case, however, "roots" sounded too grand. What could he possibly find in a town where he had no relatives and where the past his family had shared—unhappily, but briefly—was lost in the mists of time? His birthplace was another town, but he was estranged from his late mother's relatives and saw no reason to go there. To be honest, no place he'd lived in during his peripatetic childhood still had a claim on him. Home was wherever he'd happened to live, and he still felt that way. A Nowhere Man, he liked to call himself sometimes, only half-jokingly. This town, not being far from the city he had to go to for the conference, seemed like a good place to break his journey, now that there was some time to kill.

After paying the cab driver, Anil opened the gate and rolled his suitcase along the narrow path of a courtyard filled with sweet-smelling jasmine creepers, other flowers he couldn't identify, and a holy basil plant in a brick receptacle. When was the last time he'd seen a tulsi plant displayed in this manner? Not since his childhood, probably. Yellow wicker chairs were neatly arranged on the veranda between thick round columns that held up a sloping red-tiled roof. A weathered stone elephant eyed him warily. The tall, old-fashioned teak door and the steps leading up to it, with decorative arches on the sides, also reminded him of an earlier time.

It was more up-to-date inside, starting with the stylish and artfully arranged handmade furniture in the lobby, where a smiling young woman sat behind a computer screen. She said hello, brightly. The lighting was sleek, ample, and the maroon carpet below his feet felt plush. Framed paintings showing imaginary village scenes bracketed a slogan that read "Modern Comfort in a Traditional Setting." A couple of bigger hotels he'd seen that morning looked new from the outside, their bold architecture reflecting the town's desire to be seen as prosperous and happening, rather than provincial. The Devi Residency appeared to be making the same point, although in a different way.

Realizing that the town he'd lived in had largely disappeared, Anil wondered if there was anything else here that would be as recognizable to him as the Devi Residency. He doubted it. Following years of frenetic growth, the transformation was so dramatic that even the railway station, which Anil had passed through several times, looked unfamiliar. And yet, he continued to refer to it as a town. After a restless train journey, he was eager to rest for a bit and take a shower. Declining the offer of breakfast, he asked the smiling young woman if she knew anything about the building's past. Apologetically, she said no, explaining that she'd begun working there only recently. The manager, who hadn't come in yet, may know something, she added. Thanking her, he took his key and headed to the room for what he hoped would be a short nap.

The phone jangled. Waking with a start, he took a quick look at the glowing clock beside him as he grabbed the receiver. He'd slept for over two hours. Groggily, he said hello.

"Anil? So sorry if I disturbed you. This is Russy Mistry." The man spoke with a clipped accent and his deep, rumbling voice was authoritative but not gruff.

"No, not at all. I overslept, so I'm glad you called. I wanted to get in touch with you."

"I'm wondering if we can meet now rather than later. Can you come to the Coffee Club, which is right across from the Devi? I'm coming that way. There's a funeral I have to attend." The colonel wryly added, "That's not an unusual outing for me these days."

The Devi was on a side street—and because here it wasn't busy like the nearby main road, from where he could hear the rumble of traffic, Anil had no trouble crossing to the other side. The Coffee Club, he noticed, hadn't succumbed to the trendiness of Café Nation, a popular chain that drew young Wi-Fi addicts who sat hunched over their devices and fizzy, pricey drinks. At the Coffee Club, where a man was sitting near the cash register in the front, little seemed to have changed in two decades. Anil found a table easily. The customers, mostly older, were gossiping as middle-aged, uniformed waiters wearing white topis brought steaming cups of beverages and plates filled with snacks. Not only was Wi-Fi absent, Anil failed to see even one device when he looked around.

The Coffee Club was so close to the Devi that, before walking over, Anil had been able to shave and shower. Now he was ready for his coffee. Putting his notebook and pen down, Anil was skimming through the menu a waiter had given him, when he saw an elderly man enter the place. Col. Mistry, he thought. His posture erect as he walked, and looking dapper in a crisp white shirt that matched the color of his neatly combed hair, he came straight towards Anil—apparently, the colonel also had no trouble locating him—and shook his hand vigorously.

"Today I have to attend a funeral, and tomorrow I'm going out of town for a wedding," he said, sitting down. "There's never a dull day, even at my age."

"Hope I'm not imposing, Col. Mistry. I heard that you still lead a busy life."

"Not as busy as the friend who is getting married." His eyes glinted and a smile puckered his cheeks. "I'm happy to spend time with you, so no worries. Please call me Russy. My friend, by the way, is not much younger than I am. I said, 'Hey, how come you're getting married now? What made her say yes?' Can you guess what he said?"

"I won't even try."

"He said, 'She had no choice . . . I made her pregnant.'" The colonel guffawed and struck his hand on the table, drawing the attention of a few customers. He picked up the menu.

After placing their order, the colonel regaled Anil with more anecdotes, ending each one with laughter—and then, abruptly, asked what he hoped to achieve during his visit.

"Nothing . . . I have no agenda," Anil said, a little flustered. "I just wanted to visit." Why had he come? What was he trying to recapture in a town that had become so unrecognizable.

"That's fine. You don't need an agenda. I was just curious because . . . well, because you had no contact with your father. It's been so long. Do you remember anything? For instance, do you remember going to this building where you're staying? You went with your mother as a child. I know only because your father mentioned it."

"Yes, it did look familiar! That's why I chose the Devi—and, to be honest, that's what drew me to the town. What was it before?"

Putting his cup down, the colonel smiled mysteriously and dabbed his lips with a napkin. "You know, your mother was a courageous lady," he said, not answering the question. "That visit helped her make the decision—and it wasn't an easy one for her back then."

"You're referring to the divorce, of course," Anil said, leaning forward.

"Yes. You can imagine how hard it was to walk away from the marriage, given the stigma in her community. Her own parents didn't support the decision, and she lacked the qualifications for a good job. Thankfully, her brother—your uncle—stood by her. With a young child, it must have been very difficult for her."

It was, and that's probably why Anil hadn't bothered—or cared—to get in touch with his father or find out more about him. But with his parents gone, that was all in the past now.

Anil was about to speak, when he saw the colonel glance at his watch and stand up. "So sorry, dear boy," he said. "I have to go. Let's meet again. How about dinner this evening?"

Why was the colonel being so secretive about the building? Did he want Anil to make an effort to remember something? Anyway, he might as well wait till this evening. It was bound to come up during dinner. Anil, too, stood up and said he'd be happy to see him again.

The colonel turned to leave, but then stopped and, looking at Anil with piercing eyes, said, "Do you have any recollection of Baba Bala?"

"The name is vaguely familiar."

"Think about it . . . we can talk later." Smiling again, enigmatically, the colonel said goodbye and walked out in the same purposeful manner.

The colonel was a native of this town—his father and Anil's paternal grandfather had been friends—but he'd been away for many years when he was in the military, and only recently, following his retirement and the death of his wife, had he moved back. While in active service, he'd visited the town periodically to see his parents. And though he and Anil's father had been acquaintances rather than friends, the colonel apparently knew enough about his family and what had happened between his parents all those years ago.

Anil sat down and, before beckoning the waiter, looked at the menu again. Hungry now, he wanted to eat something and have another cup of coffee. After the waiter took his order, Anil opened his notebook to a blank page, picked up his pen and slowly began writing.

Will I be able to, as I'm scribbling here, recall what happened all those years ago? I didn't think so until now, having lived in this town for only a few years as a child. But the colonel's mention of Baba Bala has triggered a memory and I'm going to put my thoughts down as they come to me. The very act of writing, I think, helps us uncover what's hidden. Are the details going to be exactly correct, with all the i's dotted and the t's crossed? Obviously not. What's factual may become blurry sometimes, given the passage of time—but that doesn't make it fictional or false, I'd argue. Anyway, I'll stop rambling and get on with the story, as I know it.

My father was an alcoholic, and though I'm not sure whether it was his drinking that led to his job loss, what I do know is that his problem became worse—and my parents' relationship deteriorated—after he began spending a lot of time at home. There was much fighting, which meant shouting, using harsh language, throwing things—only to be followed by days of tense silence. Was there physical abuse, too? I cannot say—maybe I'm unable to retrieve certain episodes because they were too painful. What I do remember is being sent away sometimes for short periods to stay with relatives. But the uneasy truce I witnessed on my return didn't last.

While many things from those years remain a blur, as I write, the words "Baba Bala" have magically unlocked a door, and I feel I'm in a darkened theater to watch a scene unfold on the big screen. At first, as I open my eyes and look around, I'm confused. Then I realize I'm in my room, hiding under my bed as if I'm playing hide-and-seek. But, no, I'm not playing; I'm cowering in fear because my parents are fighting viciously in another room. Following a crashing sound, a door slams—and then, silence. The door to my room creaks open and my mother walks in, sobbing. Her feet are visible, but I remain silent when she calls out my name.

"Where are you?" she hisses. I finally crawl out and stand in front of her. Her eyes are red and she looks sad, not angry. "Come, let's go," she says softly, taking my hand.

There's no explanation as we walk briskly to the street corner, which functions as an informal autorickshaw stand, with enough room for three or four vehicles. A driver we know springs to his feet and asks my mother if she needs to go somewhere. She nods and soon we're off, with a cool breeze blowing in our faces. Having rained the previous night, the road—not so crowded because it's Sunday morning—looks cleansed and the temperature is lower than usual. There's enough sunlight, however, making objects sparkle. But my mother's mood is somber and I feel guilty about enjoying this unexpected trip that has taken us away from the gloomy house. Though silent all the way, she doesn't let go of my hand.

We reach our destination—and yes, it's the future Devi Residency. A lot would change, but the building looks much the same from the outside, with its sloping red-tiled roof, round columns and large wooden door. I see the compound, which has one well-tended tulsi plant surrounded by unruly flowering shrubs. The area around the private house—for that's what it seems to be—is open, sparsely populated, and the road going past it is unpaved.

We're in the countryside, I realize, and it's not that far from where we live. How different this area is going to look years from now. But the stone elephant watching me, as I walk with my mother along the narrow path, is not going anywhere. Even before my mother knocks on the door, it opens, as if somebody was expecting her. I'm mistaken. The woman facing us seems surprised, and she's not smiling. She must have seen us through the window.

"Did you make an appointment?" she says. "We're not taking more visitors today."

"No, I did not," my mother says. "I thought it would be okay to come now."

"Earlier, it was okay, but now we get too many visitors." The woman sighs, and I can see that she's exasperated rather than unfriendly. Perhaps she has to say this repeatedly.

"Please . . . it's urgent," my mother pleads, teary-eyed. "I don't know when I can come again. I'm willing to wait."

Embarrassed, I look away. Now I wish I hadn't come with my mother.

Unexpectedly, the woman relents. My mother's demeanor must have made a difference, because she says, "Okay, you can come in—but when you ask your question, make it quick."

My mother nods, gratefully, and we follow the woman into what looks like a waiting area. The room is airy but barely furnished, with only a couple of long benches for people to sit. Little do I know how, years from now, the inside of this house would be transformed, even as the outside would largely remain the same. The stone floor has a few cracks and the stained wall needs a fresh coat of paint. The stately old house probably belonged to a rich family with a feudal past—but clearly, it has seen better days. Several people are either sitting or standing, and while a few are talking in low voices, the rest are staring at the floor or the wall, looking anxious.

A family is summoned, just as we find a place to stand, and I see them enter another room. That's when I spot a picture of Baba Bala by the door. The framed black-and-white portrait is so big that I'm surprised I didn't notice it right away. He has a longish grey beard, but not much hair on his head—and as he is staring at the camera, with only a hint of a smile, I can tell that his dark hypnotic eyes are his most prominent feature. I wonder why the people gathered here, including my mother, want to see this man so badly.

In a curious lapse, I cannot remember if I actually saw Baba Bala. My mother must have been summoned, and I must have gone in with her to see him. But my memory is playing tricks, unfortunately, and what follows is a blur—a blank, really—as if the recording has malfunctioned, leaving a gap in the film. Or it could be an erasure. Did Baba Bala sit in a throne-like chair, as depicted in the picture, and gaze imperiously at the supplicants who came to see him? I couldn't say. I also have no idea what my mother asked, and what he said in response.

Anyway, the next thing I recall is our return journey by autorickshaw, with my tight-lipped mother still looking grim beside me. I'm filled with dread when I hear my father emerge from his room as my mother is unlocking the front door.

"Where were you?" he says. His eyes are bloodshot and his gait a little unsteady. "I didn't know where the boy was. You didn't tell me—"

"I went to see Baba Bala," she says tersely, trying to go past him.

"That fraud!" My father laughs, startling me. "I don't know what you see in him. Maybe he's a letch, too. How do you know he's not trying to bed you? Or maybe—"

"Have you no shame?" My mother is quaking with anger. "How dare you talk to me like that in front of him? Why can't you provide for the family if you're such a big protector?"

A battle has erupted, I think, but my father doesn't respond. Before turning away to go back to his room, he glances at me. Although it's hard to describe his expression—"stricken" comes closest—whenever I try to remember him, no other expression seems more vivid.

Putting the pen down, Anil closed his notebook and leaned back. He hadn't been writing for long; still, he found this unaccustomed exercise in autobiographical writing emotionally draining. After paying his bill, Anil walked back to the Devi and asked the receptionist if he could use the other computer in the lobby. She gave him the password. When a web browser popped up on the screen, he typed the words "Baba Bala."

Back in the room a little later, while Anil was untying his shoelaces, the phone rang.

It was the colonel. "I paid my respects, but the funeral made me thirsty," he said. "A *chota* peg was a big help, if you know what I mean. So, do you remember anything now?"

"This used to be Baba Bala's house, and I came here as a child with my mother."

"Aha . . . so you figured it out. Do you know what happened to him?"

"Yes. I googled him."

That visit to Baba Bala's house, all those years ago, turned out to be fateful—Anil's parents separated soon afterwards, and he and his mother began living with his uncle. The charismatic guru's rise, according to the article Anil read on the hotel computer, had been spectacular—as was his fall. Around the time Anil's mother took him for a visit, he'd been drawing wider attention with his talks, which he called discourses, and the advice he dispensed to anybody who came to see him. Free at first, these consultations became more exclusive as his popularity grew. Anil wondered if his mother was among the last people to see him before they began soliciting donations—or a booking fee, one could say—for appointments.

Not long after their visit, Baba Bala moved to a newer, larger property that became a commune, drawing followers who chose to cut ties with their families and live there. Although donations poured in from some wealthy devotees, the success didn't last. From the beginning, Anil read, there were rumors of sexual improprieties—rumors that were aggressively quashed by Baba Bala's staff. But dogged reporting by a well-known newspaper, coupled with the willingness of victims to share their complaints publicly, led to Baba Bala's downfall.

Another article detailed how, after Baba Bala's arrest, the commune broke up and its residents dispersed. It didn't say anything about the house Anil had visited with his mother, but it was clear that none of the followers stuck around to defend or promote Baba Bala. Many of his followers probably didn't take long to find other gurus. While Baba Bala did spend some time in prison, there was no word on what happened to him after his release. His disappearance from the scene, it seemed to some observers, was as dramatic as his appearance.

"Interesting," the colonel said. "Even though it happened decades ago, I guess you can read about it online without much difficulty. I don't use the computer much, I must admit. A friend had encouraged your mother to visit Baba Bala and seek his counsel. I heard all this later. She was not a follower, you see. But she was going through a rough time and needed help. In those days, it wasn't easy for somebody like your mother—"

"So you think Baba Bala advised her to leave my father and begin a new life?"

"That's what I thought, but we underestimated your mother. She wasn't gullible. Actually, Baba Bala advised her to work things out with your father—because, as he said, a woman should stay with her husband and keep the family together."

"And she did the opposite of what he told her to do," Anil said.

"Exactly! Your mother wasn't highly educated, but she was ahead of her time. Your father . . . I came to know your father in later years, after he sobered up. He wasn't a bad person, but he was—how should I say it?—weak. It was a mismatch. Do you want to see where he lived? That area has changed, of course. Somebody else lives there now, but they won't mind."

"Sure. Thank you. I should have contacted my father. I have my regrets."

"Well, that's understandable. We all have our regrets. Let me give you my address."

WHAT SID KNEW

He avoided social media or even socializing offline—and his personal information, as far as he knew, wasn't listed on any website. The name he used now, moreover, was different from what he'd been called in the old country. So when the phone rang that evening and he picked it up, unthinkingly, it was jarring to hear his former name. He took a deep breath. How stupid of him to answer the phone when the caller ID showed an unfamiliar number!

"You have the wrong number," he said, a little sharply.

The mischievous, deep-throated laugh he heard was so distinctive that he immediately knew who it was, although they hadn't spoken in ages.

"Sorry, I used the wrong name, didn't I? I should say Siddharth—or Sid. How are you? Do you know who this is?"

"Mitra."

"Yes . . . I'm glad you haven't forgotten me. You know, sometimes I introduce myself as Friend. When I get a quizzical look, I say that's what my name means." Mitra chuckled. "Do you want to know how your long-lost friend tracked you down?"

Sid did, but he also wanted to end the conversation. He'd never been that close to Mitra, and was baffled by this unexpected call. He was annoyed as well. What was Mitra doing here—and why, after all these years, had he taken the trouble to find him?

"I ran into your uncle at a wedding," Mitra added, not waiting for a response. "When he found out I was coming here, he told me about you and gave me your phone number."

Incensed, Sid wondered why his uncle had blown his cover. Out of pettiness? Following the death of Sid's parents, there had been little contact between Sid and the family, and the only reason his uncle knew where he lived was because the details of the assets bequeathed by Sid's parents were still being worked out. While his uncle had a stake in the ancestral property, so did Sid and his siblings—and they didn't agree on how it should be handled. Sid was indifferent, but he didn't want to oppose the plans of his siblings. His uncle, being on the other side of the dispute, wasn't happy. The stalemate didn't bother Sid, as long as they left him alone. He'd be happy to sign the documents when the decision was made—and cut his ties to the family.

Sid's relatives had been stunned by his sudden decision to drop out—or, as one cousin put it, go into hiding. Have you become a monk? Are you a fugitive? Have you gone crazy? These were some of the queries (and taunts) Sid got from people he knew before he stopped using email. Giving up the phone, even one without "smart" features, was harder—and so the landline became, as he saw it, his tenuous link to the world he'd distanced himself from.

"So, how come you're such a recluse?" Mitra said, and then laughed as if to reassure him. "I don't need an explanation, but if possible, I'd like to meet you. I have something to give you . . . it's a small package from your uncle."

"Where are you calling from?"

"Right here . . . in Shady Creek. I'm visiting my niece. I'll be here a few more days."

Sid remembered why, all those years ago, he hadn't felt close to Mitra, even though they'd come from the same town to attend college in the big city. At their hostel, Mitra hadn't been shy about letting on that he came from a wealthy family, that going on foreign trips and dining at fine restaurants or buying expensive things wasn't a big deal. Had Sid, who came from a family of modest means, been overly judgmental because of his insecurities? Perhaps. What Sid had found intimidating was not Mitra's nice clothes, but his poise and polished accent.

Sid knew Mitra was waiting for an invitation to what he probably thought of as a home in a suburb that, while not upscale like Shady Creek, was pleasantly middle-class, with manicured lawns and tidy double-story houses lining safe streets. How surprised he'd be to see Sid's shoddy, modest dwelling—which he was renting—on a drab, potholed street in an unfashionable part of town. But Mitra, as he scoured the stained walls, would probably be too polite to say: What happened, Sid? After all these years in this country, how come you're living like this?

Sid didn't invite him, and he didn't ask what his uncle had sent. "Sorry for the inconvenience, Mitra," he said. "I wish Uncle had contacted me before—"

"No worries . . . it's not a big item. I was happy to bring it."

Sid sensed that Mitra wasn't telling him what it was because he really wanted to see him, and maybe learn—as his uncle might have said—what Sid was up to and why his life had taken such an unexpected turn. Sending a package was just a way to get more information. What did it contain, anyway? Old family photos, perhaps, or letters and mementos from decades past.

"By the way," Mitra continued, "my niece is having a little get-together tomorrow evening. She asked me to invite you. Can you come? I'd love to see you before I leave—and give you the package, of course."

"Sure," Sid said, relieved that he didn't have to invite him. "What time?"

When Sid set out for Shady Creek the following day, with a sheet of written directions beside him, it began to rain, the globular drops crashing on his windshield before turning into twisting rivulets. Going past the wooded, fenced-in properties and McMansions visible from Shady Creek's winding and wet streets, Sid reduced his speed so that he wouldn't miss the turn. The rain intensified, blurring his vision. He braked, letting the car crawl, although there was little traffic. The wipers swished furiously and his small, ageing car shook, but Sid wasn't worried, knowing that such downpours in the area usually didn't last long.

Sid experienced his first "death alert," as he later named it, about two years ago. The feeling—and that's all it was, if anybody wanted an explanation—had been so strong that it unnerved him. He could still recall, with the force of a gale, how shocked he'd been when his premonition turned out to be true.

Sid and his girlfriend at the time had gone to a restaurant to celebrate his promotion. When he felt sick the next day, he attributed it to food poisoning, even though his girlfriend wasn't affected. He went back to the office after a brief absence, still feeling disoriented, and greeted everybody. Jokingly, Sid's boss asked if he saw the promotion as an excuse to goof off. Sid laughed, but as he looked at his boss—who was smiling and seemed to be in robust health—he felt a sudden chill. Sid couldn't account for the presentiment, the alert that felt like an internal BREAKING NEWS flash informing him of the danger ahead. The only thing missing was a high-pitched alarm. Sid's boss was in good spirits, with no knowledge of the fate awaiting him, making it harder for Sid to deliver the news. How could he say something so terrible, anyway? It would be bizarre, to say the least. But even though Sid kept it to himself, he couldn't avoid the dread of knowing—in his bones—that his boss would be dead in a week. How did he know? He couldn't say, but that didn't make the sense of foreboding less real. His boss was a doomed man.

Taking on a new project that involved travel, Sid was grateful for the chance to get away from the office and not see his boss for the next few days. When he got back, his boss was out of town to see a client. It was a lucky break, allowing Sid to avoid him altogether and not think about what was coming. The long hours he put in kept his mind gainfully employed, but his fear and guilt—and sorrow—didn't abate. Should he tell anybody about the boss's impending death? That would be absurd, irrational—how could he or anybody else know when somebody was going to die? His confidant would laugh at him or, worse, think he's crazy. Besides, if it was preordained, there wasn't anything one could do to prevent it, was there?

Nine days after the alert, as Sid was checking his email late at night, there was a terse note to all the employees. Tragically, it said, Sid's boss had suffered a fatal heart attack at home. The family was in shock and mourning privately, but details would follow soon. Sid was so shaken by the news that he couldn't sleep that night. And the next morning, he had to force himself to get out of bed. It turned out to be the most painful, miserable day of his life.

The alerts didn't stop. They would come suddenly, often when he was with that person. Invariably, it was somebody he'd known a long time. It was spooky, filling him with shame that he couldn't do anything. In the case of his girlfriend, the date of death was years away. But that gave him little comfort. They'd talked about getting married and having children, but he now realized it would be a mistake. Dismaying though it was to know when she'd be leaving this world, imagine the horror of having the same information about his children. Much as he loved her, the only life possible for him was the single life.

Once when he tried to warn a friend, obliquely, about his impending death, the man was so unsettled by Sid's disclosure that he ended up overdosing on drugs. He did recover, but that didn't prevent him from dying later in the year, around the designated date, which Sid had known months in advance. Cause: Unknown. His family didn't share any details and they chose to skip the autopsy. After this incident, Sid decided to keep such ghoulish knowledge to himself. Telling people didn't make a difference, in any case. It was better to shield them from such devastating news and let them enjoy—in peace and happiness, he hoped—the remaining time they had on the earth.

Sid didn't reveal his dark secret when his girlfriend asked why he appeared so anxious, so withdrawn. Something seemed to be worrying him, even haunting him, she said. Was he feeling okay? Sid nodded. What galled him the most was that these doomed people had, as far as he knew, no way of extending their lives. Their departure dates were set in stone, as was his—although, in a quirk that bothered him, Sid's date of death remained a mystery to him, adding to his sense of guilt and wretchedness. Though relieved, in a way, Sid found it cruelly ironic.

The torment didn't stop, forcing Sid to see a doctor—or rather, a few doctors. But they found nothing wrong with him even after several tests. "Physically, you're okay, so that's good news," his primary physician said, reviewing the medical report. "Now I think you should see a psychiatrist. I'll give you a referral."

Sid thanked him and said he'd follow up—but he never did. Sid's girlfriend had been pleased by his decision to seek medical help, although he didn't tell her the real reason. When, without any explanation, he went back to living as before, her concern and alarm turned into anger. Finally, in what he later saw as a misguided—if inevitable—attempt to save their foundering relationship, he told her what was really going on with him.

She stared at him in stunned disbelief, as if he'd gone mad.

"Do you mean to say you know when I'm going to die?" she said, sounding hoarse.

"Yes, sadly—but you have nothing to worry, dear. You'll live a long time. I don't want to tell you how long."

She started crying. "Sid, you need help . . . I don't know what's happening . . . "

It didn't take long afterwards for the relationship to end—and once it did, Sid lost interest in his job, where things hadn't been the same since his boss's untimely death. Sid quit his job and moved away. While he didn't necessarily avoid people, he did avoid forming attachments. Any woman or man he got to know well enough would become, to him, a ticking time bomb. And he knew there was no way he could defuse it. He didn't want that burden.

Seeking psychiatric help wouldn't solve anything, Sid knew, because he wasn't delusional. His predictions, if that was the right word, had come true without exceptions—and in a couple of cases, including his father's death, he had known the exact date. It was uncanny. A week before his father died, Sid had flown into the country without informing anybody. Although his father was ailing, nobody had expected him to die so abruptly—except Sid.

Sid stepped on the accelerator, just as the rain eased off, and turned right onto a street lined with newer houses, standing a little closer together and fronted by well-tended yards that looked freshly washed. Several cars were parked on the shoulder. Sid didn't pull over—he saw no need for that and wondered why he had even bothered to come. What was Mitra going to give him? Anyway, as he knew, the real goal was to reestablish contact. But Sid had nothing to say, and he didn't want to know when Mitra or anybody else was going to die. Coming here was a mistake. He should have given Mitra an excuse—but while it was too late for that, it wasn't too late to avoid the visit. Pressing the accelerator, Sid went past the house and kept driving.

AT CROSS PURPOSES

MIGRANT

The loud ring, waking Gopal in the middle of the night, was so unexpected that at first it didn't seem real. Then, reaching for his phone, he wondered if something terrible had happened somewhere to somebody he knew. An accident, perhaps, or a death. But when he pressed the button to talk, all he got was the dial tone. Was it a misdial, then, or a dream? When he heard the ring again—distinctly, jarringly—it chilled him to the bone, and for the first time Gopal wished he had a gun. Unbelievably, it was the doorbell. After lying still for what felt like a long time, paralyzed by uncertainty, he got out of bed and walked gingerly to the living room. Strange as it might sound, given his misgivings, he was ready to open the front door.

But he was jumping ahead. To understand what happened next, Gopal would have to go back and talk about Sam's Diner. It was called Sam's, almost always, just as its owner, Sampat, was simply known as Sam. An affable bear of a man, with twinkling dark eyes and a stylish drooping moustache that accentuated his rakish looks, he was a decade older than Gopal. While they weren't close friends, Gopal got to know him fairly well because, as a bachelor who disliked cooking, he ate regularly at his restaurant.

Sam was gregarious and attentive, never failing to greet diners and ask how they liked the food. He remembered not just the names of his loyal customers but also the dishes they preferred, which sometimes appeared magically on their table even before they'd spoken to a waiter. It seemed as if he knew most of the people worth knowing in their township, whose main artery went past the restaurant and led to a multilane highway, where you could see—if you stood on the commuter rail station's platform and looked down—a glittering river of steel surging towards the city. Like many residents, Gopal avoided the highway and took the train to work.

It didn't take long for Gopal to realize that Sam's extra attention went to folks who had some standing in the community, and it was on *their* tables these special, unasked-for dishes appeared. He often embraced these customers, even hovering near their table in case they needed anything—and there was more than a touch of fawning in his usually charming manner.

"It's good to know these people," Sam once said, with a satisfied chuckle, after a county official—Gopal couldn't remember what his job was—left the restaurant. "You never know when somebody like him will come in handy. You and I are in the same boat."

"What do you mean? As migrants?"

"We're immigrants, my friend, not migrants! We came on a plane. Migrants are the folks I employ. Now, *they* came on a boat, a real boat."

Gopal knew exactly what he meant but didn't say anything. Focusing on his plate, he was relieved when he heard a voice greet Sam, pulling him away from his table. A customer had just walked in.

A word about the food, which was naturally a big reason for the restaurant's popularity. Sam's was like no other eatery Gopal knew, specializing in quirky fusion dishes that were a hodgepodge of cuisines and cultures. They had, he thought, outrageous names—but it all worked, somehow, and several dishes were outrageously good. For instance, you could order Wasabi Noodle Samosas as an appetizer, Pesto Chicken Kabob Tacos or Fish Vindaloo Burritos with Kimchi as an entrée, Baked Masala Fries with Chili Mayo as a side, and Spicy Chai Vanilla Ice Cream with Lychees as the dessert. The prices, fortunately for Gopal, were not outrageous.

Sam's employees had worked on ships, mostly in the kitchen, before ending up at his restaurant. He wasn't easy to work for, but the pay was decent, which perhaps explained why they stayed. Always gracious as a host, Sam could be mercurial as a boss; not infrequently, his temper flared when he was in the back. But while his impatience with employees wasn't hard to miss, he could also be quite friendly—and generous. When there was a need, he loaned or even gave money from his pocket. Occasionally, he took his staff on a shopping expedition, and if one of them got sick, he accompanied him to the doctor's clinic.

Sam, as far as Gopal could tell, never berated his workers in front of customers. Except once—which came as a shock when he witnessed it. First, though, it was worth mentioning how Gopal met the young man who faced Sam's wrath. After dining at the restaurant one day, he was driving back to his apartment, only five minutes away, when he spotted Imran on the sidewalk, heading in the same direction. He was an employee in the kitchen—and though Gopal had seen him a few times at Sam's, they hadn't spoken yet. There was some daylight left, but it was quickly fading, as was the crepuscular charm of the fall evening. Switching his headlights on, he pulled over to the curb.

Turning his head in surprise, he saw Gopal and broke into a smile.

"Imran, right? Going home? I can drop you."

He hesitated. "No problem. Not far. I can walk. Thank you."

Gopal could have ended the conversation there and kept going. Imran had recognized him, obviously, but for some reason he was reluctant to accept his offer. Instead of leaving, Gopal asked him where he lived, a question that seemed to unsettle Imran.

"Going to store," he said, pointing. "Not going home."

Gopal, with a smile and a wave, pulled away. He was almost in his apartment, still mulling over the encounter, when it struck him that Imran didn't want him to find out where he lived. Maybe he was embarrassed? Clearly, despite his claim, Imran hadn't been going to the supermarket—because, as a pedestrian, he'd have known to turn by now and take the easier, shorter path that led to the shopping center.

Gopal's one-bedroom apartment, in the residential complex behind the shopping center, had such a small kitchen that he scarcely bothered to cook, relying instead on takeout and Sam's, which frequently became his hangout for reading or doing computer work, not just for eating and drinking. Sam usually stopped by his table to chat with him. Inevitably, after a few minutes, he got drawn to other customers, some of whom, being as outgoing as he was, greeted him heartily and made small talk. Though married—happily, Gopal figured—and a father, Sam liked to flirt with attractive women. But he did it so unthreateningly that they didn't seem to mind, at least outwardly.

Twice, without any warning, Sam tried to introduce Gopal to young, presumably unattached women. His efforts fell flat, with awkward smiles and puzzled expressions—and to Gopal's relief, he didn't repeat the experiment.

"I didn't know this was a singles bar," Gopal said.

Sam laughed. "You're a young man, but I always see you with a book," he said. "You should go out more, my friend, and meet girls."

After his encounter with Imran, Gopal saw him work as a waiter—twice. The first time, Sam was also in the restaurant, processing a credit card payment at the cash register, when there was a loud crash. Turning just in time to see a plate slice through the air like a missile, barely missing a diner,

Gopal also heard a large bowl shatter on the floor, its contents splattering messily. Imran was on the floor, too, looking bewildered. Silence descended, as everybody watched, only to be broken by an outburst from Sam.

"*Saala* . . . clumsy, useless ass!" he said, rushing towards Imran. "You want to injure my customers? Don't you watch where you're going? Get up and clean the mess."

Then, shifting his attention, Sam apologized profusely to the family, who seemed shocked more by his reaction than the accident. Indeed, so was Gopal, never having seen Sam lose his cool in front of customers. It was puzzling, uncharacteristic of him. Any shouting was done behind closed doors—behind the scenes, as it were, away from the neatly choreographed action of the decorous front section, where the customers dined quietly. He must have been having a bad day.

Imran got up—nobody asked if he was okay—and, picking up the dishes, went to get the mop and bucket. Feeling tense, Gopal left without placing an order. They were busy, anyway, and the thought of reading his book while he waited for his food was no longer appealing. Opening his car door in the parking lot, he looked up when the honks of Canada geese caught his attention. The large, noisy birds had long black necks and brownish bodies, and they were flying low as they made their way across the evening sky, which was a bold mix of gold and grey, while the sun, now a fiery red ball, began to sink rapidly in the distance.

Gopal didn't know much about birds, but he remembered reading how Canada geese formed a V-shape during their fall migration, not unlike a squadron of jets in the sky. The article also said that changes in temperature and light triggered bird migrations, as did the need for sustenance. Did birds also migrate when the ecosystem changed? Probably. In the case of humans, major upheavals—caused by civil war, for instance—did trigger large-scale migrations.

Imran seemed considerably younger than the other employees, but appearances were deceptive and it was quite possible that, as one of the "boat people," to use Sam's ugly term, he had worked on a ship before coming here.

Oddly enough, the next time Gopal came to the restaurant, Imran seemed more eager to talk to him. Sam wasn't around, and Imran was again helping out in the front.

"Did you like food, Mr. Gopal," he said, clearing Gopal's table after he ate. "Can I get anything else?"

"It was good. Thanks. I'll have some coffee."

"No problem. I bring now. Mr. Gopal, can I ask something if you have time?"

"Of course. You can just call me Gopal."

Imran smiled and nodded, but he still didn't use the name without the prefix. He asked for help with a letter, puzzling Gopal at first. Then Imran explained that he wanted to put his work experience down on paper and draft a letter. Gopal assumed that he wanted to apply for other jobs. Would Sam approve? Gopal wasn't sure, but he had no qualms about helping Imran. Scribbling his address on a napkin, he told him that he could come to his apartment in the evening.

But he didn't come. Correction. Imran did show up—although the hour was so late that it was the middle of the night when the doorbell rang, arousing Gopal and filling him with dread. Once Gopal got over the initial jitters, he went to the living room to investigate. His adrenalin must have kicked in, for he switched the light on and boldly said, "Who's there?"

A burglar wouldn't make sense, so was it a drunk or a juvenile delinquent? Gopal didn't feel brave, to be honest, and his right hand, holding the phone, trembled slightly as he got ready to dial 9-1-1. But then he heard a familiar voice.

"Sir, Imran here. So sorry for disturbing . . . for coming now."

Gopal felt a flurry of emotions: annoyance, bewilderment, apprehension. "This is a very odd time," he said with irritation. "Why did you come now?"

"Something happened . . . at restaurant." Imran hesitated. "Don't know where to go."

Did he want to rob him? However, despite the oddness of the situation, Gopal didn't feel threatened. And he believed him. Maybe he had an inkling all along that it was Imran, making it easier for him to overcome any hesitation about opening the door.

"Sir, it's Sam . . . "

Gopal quickly unlocked the door. Standing in the hallway, a disheveled Imran looked shaken and out of breath, as if he'd been running. From where, from whom? He looked past Gopal, anxiously, perhaps wondering if anybody else was in the apartment. His shirt was torn, as if he'd been in a scuffle, and there was a reddish bruise on his cheek.

"Sam," he said again. "We had fight . . . in restaurant. Need help."

"What! Come in and tell me what happened. I'll get some water."

Hesitantly, Imran entered the living room and looked around. Asking him to sit, Gopal went to the kitchen and got some water. Imran took a long gulp, draining the glass, and put it down with a sigh. Declining a refill, he said, "Thank you. Can we go? To Sam's. I tell as we go."

"Okay, let's go," Gopal said, picking up his car keys. He evidently had a good reason for hastening to the restaurant, and Gopal didn't want to stall him.

For a few weeks, Imran said as they walked down the stairs, he'd been sleeping in the restaurant without Sam's knowledge. The scheme was simple—Imran had managed to make a copy of the key, and he knew the security code. He left once his shift ended, only to return after the restaurant was closed. They didn't get into where he spent his time waiting or why he'd become homeless. That night, Imran had just fallen asleep in the restaurant when he suddenly heard the door open. He opened his eyes, startled, just as the lights came on.

"What the hell is going on?"

Imran, shocked, saw Sam staring at him, his face contorted in puzzlement and anger. He also seemed drunk—his eyes were bloodshot. Imran was frightened. He couldn't say why Sam had returned to the restaurant so late, after it was closed for the night. Maybe he'd forgotten something? What Imran did know, from gossip in the kitchen, was that Sam had been under stress lately because of arguments with his wife, who hadn't visited the restaurant in many days.

Things got out of control quickly. When Imran said that he was just sleeping there temporarily, until he could find new accommodations, Sam lost it and lunged forward, calling him a "lying, thieving, cheating bastard." Imran backed away and tried to speak again.

"Worthless scum . . . how did you manage to sneak in?" Sam yelled, advancing again.

Trying to fend him off, Imran held his shoulder and pushed him. That only enraged Sam, who swung his fist. Struck in the face, Imran staggered backwards—and, as his body touched the table behind him, he unintentionally reached for the knife lying there. He'd kept the kitchen knife close by at night, but it was just a precaution. Robberies were uncommon in that area.

Seeing the knife, Sam spat out, "Think I'm of scared you . . . you slimy son of a—?"

"No . . . no . . . ," Imran said, quickly removing his hand from the knife. But it was too late. As Sam flung himself on him, it devolved into a full-fledged fight—although without the knife, thankfully. It all happened so fast that Imran, still in a daze, couldn't quite say how Sam got knocked out. From what Gopal could gather, Sam passed out after he struck his head on the floor.

Imran panicked. Saying Sam's name, Imran sprinkled some water on Sam's face and shook him, but Sam didn't open his eyes. Imran didn't know what to do and was afraid of calling anybody. He didn't say why, though Gopal assumed it was because he lacked proper documentation.

"You could have called Sam's home," he said.

"Yes," Imran replied, not looking at him. "But afraid . . . Did not know what to say."

Then, remembering Gopal, Imran said, he shut the door of the restaurant and ran all the way to his apartment. They had by now reached Sam's in the car, and from the road they could see a police cruiser parked close to the restaurant. Its lights were flashing, but Gopal couldn't tell if anybody was inside. Imran moaned and lowered his head, as if he was trying to hide. He seemed scared. Sam's car, they noticed, was parked near the front door.

The road's emptiness was unusual, eerie, as though they were driving through a hastily abandoned town. The absence of vehicles didn't stop the traffic lights from changing to red, dutifully, and then back to green. How everybody took things for granted. So much had to work smoothly, even at this ghostly hour, so that people could lead comfortable lives.

Did Sam regain consciousness and call the cops? Regardless of what happened, they'd have come right away when summoned by Sam. Hope he was okay, Gopal thought. Instinctively, without making a left towards the restaurant, he kept driving until they reached the next intersection. Imran didn't speak—so Gopal was right in thinking that he didn't want to go to Sam's anymore. Glancing sideways while waiting for the lights to change, he said, "Seems like there's a policeman at the restaurant."

"Don't know why . . . don't know why the police came. No major problem. Knife not used."

Alarmed, Gopal looked again at Imran's clothes, visible in the pale light of a street lamp. No, there was no blood anywhere. Well, who knew what really happened? In any case, he didn't want to make him do anything; it was entirely up to him.

"Should we go to the restaurant and check on Sam?"

"No . . . no . . . ," he said, his voice quavering. "Sir, please, can you drop at train station?"

It didn't take them long to get there. Pulling into the deserted parking lot, Gopal stopped the car and, without turning off the ignition, took out his wallet to give him some money.

THE PLOT

On the day Neel returned to his flat, he discovered that Sai had stopped talking—and eating. Moreover, having retreated to the little shed behind the building, Sai was refusing to leave what had been his home for several months. Summer hadn't arrived, so it probably wasn't sweltering in the tin-roofed shed; still, as Neel remembered from his only look inside, it was a dingy, barely furnished room that felt like a prison cell. Apart from the weak glow of a single bare bulb, the only illumination in the cramped space came from the sunlight trickling in through a small barred window. Sai was the day watchman, hired after a couple of burglaries nearby had rattled the building's residents. Since there was already a night watchman for the neighborhood, Sai's job was to stay vigilant during the day and be a handyman who could run errands.

Neel had just returned from a trip to the U.S., where he'd settled with his family as a teenager. Now, odd though it seemed, he was an expat in India, the land of his birth. While waiting to catch his connecting flight, he'd texted Murti to inform him that Sai could resume delivering the newspaper and milk to his flat. "Sai fried will do," read Murti's response, baffling Neel momentarily. Then, boarding the plane, he wondered why Sai had been fired. But instead of texting again, Neel switched off his phone, letting the thought hang in the air. Not unlike an airport announcement that sounds garbled initially, the text's meaning would become clear in due course.

It was early morning, the city still unburdened by heavy traffic or pollution, when a cab deposited Neel at the front gate of the building. The tawny sky was just beginning to brighten when Neel got out and saw that the gate was already unlocked. The man from the dairy would have brought the milk packets by now. Neel paid the driver and started rolling his suitcase on the gravelly lane, setting off a grating sound. A stray dog skulking by the compound wall approached cautiously and barked in displeasure, though the protest seemed half-hearted more than threatening. Earlier, such encounters used to unsettle him—but he'd realized that the best way to deal with it was to look away and keep walking nonchalantly.

Neel's attitude of disregarding anything upsetting, he discovered, had the curious effect of making him indifferent to his surroundings. "Desensitized" was the word in vogue. In this sprawling metropolis, you became desensitized after a while.

Neel recalled how, on his first visit to the area where his flat was located, it had been jarring to see a long row of flimsy, primitive-looking tents crowded together near a busy intersection, barely a stone's throw from a swanky mall. These tents were makeshift homes for construction workers, whose scruffy children played on the abutting road while their mothers cooked on the sidewalk. The building craze had converted what used to be uninhabited land into a bustling township, pockmarked by big ditches that sent up clouds of dust. High-rise buildings had sprung up, seemingly overnight, to house the hordes of technology workers drawn like moths to the many new jobs in the gleaming Info Tech City close by. And the boom had also attracted migrant laborers from the countryside.

The words "Sixten Tower" appeared on the gate. A typo, he'd thought at first, but it actually stood for 610, the number of the building, which was five stories high and had ten flats. Going up in the small lift, Neel heard sounds—running water, voices, footsteps—that announced the start of another day. Stepping out on the fourth floor, he was cheered by the sight of a milk packet near his front door. Yes, he could make coffee now! In the kitchen, Neel took a few refreshing sips of his hot brew and walked up to the window for a look at the little shed in the back.

Earlier, just as the cab was about to turn onto the street leading to Sixten Tower, Neel saw the night watchman waiting at a bus stop on the main road. Asking the driver to pull over for a minute, Neel rolled down the window and said, "Going home after the night shift?"

Looking up in surprise, the watchman, a Gurkha immigrant, smiled when he recognized Neel. "Yes," he said. "A lot happened while you were gone. I'm not covering Sixten anymore. They don't want me to enter the compound."

"Why not?"

"Because of Sai. He's on a hunger strike and is refusing to talk or leave the shed. He had a fight—"

A horn blared, startling them, and when Neel turned around, he saw a bus approaching the stop. As the cab driver quickly pulled away, the watchman waved and said, "I'm sure you'll find out more soon."

Holding his coffee mug, Neel gazed at the shed and wondered if he'd be able to see Sai. But the door was closed and the light didn't appear to be on. Surrounded by weeds and overgrown grass, the ramshackle shed looked abandoned. He found it hard to believe that the usually voluble and cheerful Sai was in there, observing a silent fast and refusing to move out. But why had he been fired? People liked him, as far as Neel could tell, and he seemed capable. Sure, he had a few quirks—such as his tendency to ask for "phoren" T-shirts, or bang rather than knock on the door—but then again, who wasn't quirky? To Sai's credit, he'd been eager to be helpful around the building.

The doorbell rang, to Neel's surprise. It was early for visitors. When he opened the door, Murti greeted him but didn't smile. "May I speak to you?"

"Of course. Please come in, Murti. Would you like some coffee?"

Short and slender, his thinning hair generously streaked with grey, and wearing glasses that were a little big for his face, the middle-aged visitor appeared mild-mannered—but Neel knew that Murti, as the resident manager, controlled Sixten Tower's affairs with an iron fist. Declining Neel's offer, he sat upright on the sofa and, adjusting his checked bush shirt, said, "I just wanted to update you on what happened."

"Appreciate it. I was surprised by the turn of events, because I thought Sai was a good worker and well liked by people in the building. Is he fasting to protest?"

Murti pursed his lips, looking peeved. He didn't look at Neel. "I don't know who you've been talking to, but he's a troublemaker. He's like an illegal migrant who crossed the border and is refusing to leave. The shed is not his territory."

Neel thought he was being unnecessarily dramatic, and the analogy didn't make sense—but there was no point in arguing and riling him up even more. Better to keep the tone neutral. "So what happened, Murti?" he said casually.

"What happened was he thought he was a big shot. Instead of being grateful, he became bold and arrogant. He began plotting against me. The shed was a temporary place for him to stay until he found his own accommodation. When I found out that he was making improvements, I told him to move out. He refused, so I fired him. And now we have a problem on our hands.

You know how these people are—you give them an inch, they take a mile!"

Neel shifted uncomfortably, crossing and uncrossing his legs. He didn't like Murti's tone and the direction in which this was going, dragging him into an unpleasant swamp. Neel was about to speak, but he didn't get a chance.

"Think he can blackmail us?" Murti said, his voice rising. "Rascal! It's outrageous. Tomorrow I'm having a meeting for everybody in the building. I'd like for us to find a way to get rid of him."

Murti appeared so agitated by now, with a trembling hand and flushed face, that Neel thought it best to end the visit. Saying that he'd be glad to attend the meeting and help in any way he could, Neel quickly ushered him out. Walking back to the kitchen, Neel looked down again at the ground extending to the compound wall. A lone guava tree, bent and swaying gently in the breeze, stood like a weathered old sentinel next to the shed. A couple of trees on the property had been knocked down in recent months, and Neel wondered if this remaining guava tree—which had no fruit, as if it had already given up hope—was next.

Was it true, then, that Murti & Co. were planning to erect another building? Would there really be enough space, even after tearing down the shed and perhaps the compound wall, to build anything here, adding to the congestion and putting a further strain on the water supply, which was running low and being rationed? What if the rains failed again? That wasn't going to stop them, according to Hasan, Neel's neighbor in the building. They'd be willing to dig deeper to reach the aquifer, just as they'd be willing to encroach on the neighboring land to accommodate their building.

"They'll do anything to get their way," Hasan had said. "It's all about the money, my friend. Greed is great, not God."

That seemed the most likely explanation for why Sai was being forced out. A jet-lagged Neel sat up for a long time that night, reading. Feeling restless, he rose from the sofa a few times and walked up to the kitchen window. No light came on in the shed even after darkness fell, and it was hard to believe that Sai was in there. How did he manage? Maybe Neel should have tried to contact him. But what about the others—why hadn't anybody else been able to reach out to Sai? He should have made inquiries earlier.

Hasan hadn't been in when he got back from his trip, and now everybody in the building except Neel was asleep. Perhaps Sai was sleeping, too, despite his fast. Well, Neel would have to wait till the next day. Something was bound to happen soon. The meeting, he hoped, would end the impasse. How long had it been going on, anyway?

Around three or four o'clock, he fell into a deep slumber and had a dream. A stray dog began barking loudly. It was joined by another dog, then two more, and soon the noise reached a crescendo. Neel wasn't scared because, though he was standing nearby, the dogs were not threatening him. Instead, they were barking—on and on—at the little shed, as if a burglar lurked inside. But the door remained closed and there was no response even after the dogs began scratching on it furiously.

When Neel opened his eyes, sunlight was pouring in through the window, warming his face, and he found himself slouching in the sofa, his book still resting on his chest. He had barely fifteen minutes for the meeting on the terrace. Getting ready quickly and swallowing his coffee, he took a quick peek at the shed. It still looked unoccupied, but in the daylight he noticed a few covered bowls—had he missed them yesterday?—near the door. Food, perhaps? They seemed untouched. And then, with a shock, he noticed a lock on the door. How could that be? Tearing himself away from the window, he hurried to the meeting, with questions swirling in his mind.

For a Saturday morning, the building was strangely quiet—which meant that all the residents were on the terrace, waiting for the meeting to start. The canvas-covered section of the terrace, carpeted and sparely furnished with metal chairs, acted as the building's gathering place for events. Almost everybody was there. Neel found an unoccupied chair next to Hasan, who greeted him brightly. The meeting proved to be short.

Clearing his throat, Murti said, "Ladies and gentlemen, I have an unexpected announcement." He appeared uncharacteristically nervous and was perspiring, although it was pleasant at this hour. "Sai is not in the shed," he continued. "It's empty . . . I don't know when he left. As far as I'm concerned, this is over and we can move on."

There was a stunned silence, followed by a flurry of questions. Any idea where he went? Did he leave a note or contact anybody? Is he okay? What happened?

Murti's terse answers were "No" or "I don't know." There were no immediate plans to build another building, he added, but the shed would be demolished soon. When the meeting moved on to other matters involving the residents, Neel and Hasan drifted away, as did a few others.

"So what do you think?" Hasan said when they reached their floor.

"Puzzling. I don't know what to make of it."

"Fishy is what I'd say." Opening his door, Hasan invited Neel in for a cup of tea.

Widowed and solitary, Hasan was always friendly, often giving him news about his children and grandchildren, who had settled abroad and didn't visit him much.

"What do you mean?" Neel said, entering the modestly furnished living room.

"I'll be back," Hasan replied mysteriously, heading to the kitchen, while Neel sat on a chair by the window and looked around. A small, ancient-looking television set was perched on a cardboard box, and Neel wondered if it still worked.

Emerging from the kitchen, Hasan handed him a steaming cup. "Didn't you hear the dogs barking last night?" he said. "They were loud, and it didn't stop for a while. Unusual . . . don't you think?"

Neel's heart began racing, as if a treadmill he was walking on had skipped to a higher speed. Taking a sip to calm himself, he said, "The dogs around here bark, don't they?"

"Yes, but not like this, especially at night. Nobody investigated because it was not their problem and they didn't want to be bothered. Look, I don't mean to sound paranoid, but how did the lock appear on the door? I didn't see it before. Let's just say that force can be used to get rid of unwanted people. It happens, I've heard, more often than we realize."

His face flushing as he swallowed some hot tea, Neel tried to absorb all this. "What can we do about it?" he said.

"Nothing much, I'm afraid," Hasan said. "But I'm going to call a reporter I know at the local *Daily News and Views*. Whether he's interested or not, we should let him know."

"Good idea. You know, I still cannot figure out what happened, why Sai was fired. He was cordial and a good worker, available at all hours. Wasn't he entitled to sleep on the property? Murti's reasoning was ridiculous. So what if Sai was making some minor improvements? The shed is dilapidated—"

"Indeed. Unfortunately, people like Sai don't have many options in the city. You see, his community is involved in the tanning business. Not wanting to do that kind of work, he left his hometown and came here."

A clatter outside Hasan's flat stopped their conversation. The meeting having ended, some people were coming down the stairs instead of waiting for the building's only lift, which could be temperamental.

Neel soon got busy at work with a new project. Later that week, returning late to his flat, he saw that the shed was no longer there. Murti hadn't wasted any time in tearing it down. Neel didn't speak to Hasan that night, and the following morning he left fairly early to catch a flight—although this time he was making a domestic trip to see his client. Work kept him away, and it was another week before he saw Hasan again. Neel was opening his door, after a trip to the local supermarket for groceries, when he appeared next to him, smiling.

"Hello, Neel, I see that you were gone for a few days," he said. "Well, I have some news." Although nobody else was around, Hasan seemed skittish. Dropping his voice, he added: "I called the reporter. He said something interesting. They're investigating the building."

"Because of Sai?"

"No, not because of him. There wasn't enough information, he said. There have been other such cases, with people vanishing or leaving abruptly. But unless there's solid evidence, it's hard to prove anything. He said that we should file a 'Missing Person' report with the police if we suspected anything. I said that we didn't have anything solid."

"Then why is the building being investigated?"

"Aha." There was a gleam in Hasan's eyes, and Neel could see that he was enjoying the drama, the telling of the story. "There's a corruption scandal involving properties in this area," Hasan continued. "It's the Wild West, my friend. Bribes were paid to acquire land and illegal boundaries were drawn to increase the size of plots."

"Shocking! So, perhaps, the shed was built on somebody else's property? How ironic—because it was Sai who was accused of being an illegal occupant."

"Exactly, Neel. Maybe that's why I haven't seen Murti lately. He's hunkering down, I'm sure, and busy talking to his lawyers. I can't wait to see how all this unfolds."

"Indeed, Hasan. It'll be very interesting. Would you like some tea?"

Shutting the door once Hasan entered the flat, Neel began to tell him what he'd seen on his last trip to the airport. He hadn't stopped thinking about it. Neel was in a cab, approaching a shantytown crowded with the kind of tents he'd noticed on his first visit, when there was a sudden diversion in the traffic. People holding placards were protesting loudly, but Neel couldn't get a closer look because the cab had to take a detour. He asked the driver what was going on.

"Agitation, sar," the driver said, as the cab slowed and took a sharp turn. "Labor people asking for better living conditions."

Craning his neck, Neel looked past the policemen at the demonstrators behind the barricade—and turned around only when they were out of sight. For a moment, though it was a long moment, one protester looked like Sai. He was shouting and waving a sign. Then the moment passed, and Neel wondered if he'd just imagined it. Maybe he wanted him to be Sai. Getting off to check wasn't an option. Besides, he had a plane to catch.

THE LAST STOP

This happened years ago, but if I close my eyes, I can still remember the "MISSING" flier I saw that day. I was a bachelor then, living and working in New York City, and had taken some time off to visit my sister in Atlanta. On the day before I headed back, we went to see a movie and then stopped at an Indian grocery store, where Deepa got out to pick up a couple of items. I remained in the car—until I happened to see that flier posted near the store. The missing person's face in the picture looked eerily familiar, even from a distance, prompting me to open the door and step out.

"What's the matter?" Deepa asked. I was standing outside, open-mouthed, when she emerged from the store with a bag in her hand.

"That kid . . . " I sputtered, pointing at the flier. "I've seen that boy."

"Really?" It was her turn to be astonished. "Where? Are you sure?"

"At a restaurant in Jackson Heights."

This popular Indian eatery was close to where I lived in the borough of Queens, and like some other singles in the area, I dined there regularly. The boy, sitting alone at a small table, had caught my attention because he stood out among the adults in the restaurant, which had just opened for the day. His tight-fitting clothes were crumpled, his hair disheveled, and he seemed to be about fifteen. I recalled seeing him eat his meal quickly, without looking up. Soon, the restaurant became crowded and I lost track of him.

"Well, let's call this number and inform his family," Deepa said.

"No, wait." I was suddenly overcome by doubt. "I'm not so sure. Let me find him again. He probably lives in the area, and the restaurant people may know more. We can call the family if it's really him. I don't want to disappoint them."

"You're right. They'd have reported it, anyway. Better to wait until you're sure."

The missing teen's name was Samir Something—and, as I guessed, he was a high school student, aged sixteen. About a month ago, according to the flier, he'd left his home in suburban Atlanta without telling anybody, and there had been no word from him since. Before we left, I grabbed my camera and took a picture of the flier.

Soon after landing in New York, I went to the Indian restaurant in Jackson Heights, not far from La Guardia Airport. Although the genial owner was busy, he had a moment for me. He remembered the teenager, but confessed that he hadn't seen him recently.

"He probably lives close by," he said, swiping a customer's credit card. "I've seen him walking down the street."

He was referring to 74th Street, the artery of that bustling neighborhood. Giving him my business card, before stepping out on that street, I asked him to get the teen's address, if possible, when he saw him again. Then, sauntering past the hawkers and pedestrians thronging the sidewalk, I scanned the faces around me, though I knew the chances of seeing him were slim. There had to be a better way to find him. Perhaps, after consulting the boy's family, I could post a flier. But again I became indecisive, wondering if I'd made a terrible mistake. Even if I hadn't, wouldn't the sudden publicity in the area scare him away?

On this colorful stretch of Jackson Heights, there were appliance and jewelry stores, boutiques with sari-clad mannequins in the windows, eateries, a supermarket, and stores that sold groceries, DVDs, CDs, even books. Bollywood music added to the bazaar atmosphere, as did the enticing aromas wafting from the kitchens. The next day, too, after work, I wandered aimlessly in the neighborhood, hoping to catch a glimpse of Samir.

Then, as I was heading to work that Friday, I spotted him. Changing my route, I'd walked down Roosevelt Avenue until I reached 74th Street—with the rust-colored No. 7 train, dubbed the Asian Express, rumbling above me as it carried commuters from Queens to Manhattan—and was waiting at the intersection to cross, when I saw him approach the subway station. His hair was longer and unkempt, but I recognized him instantly. My heart beating rapidly, I followed him down the stairs to the platform.

His face was impassive as he stood away from the crowd and waited for the train. Watching him discreetly, I tried to think of a casual opening that would put him at ease. He must have been deeply unhappy at home to take such a drastic step. I recalled the notices I used to see in Indian newspapers. The headline would often read "Missing" or "All is forgiven," followed by the teen's photo and a few details. "Mother is ill and waiting for you," a notice sometimes said, heartbreakingly. "Please come home soon."

Clackety-Clack . . . Clackety-Clack . . . Clackety-Clack. When the E train from Jamaica Center pulled in and screeched to a halt, the doors opened with a whoosh and waves of commuters surged in both directions. Following the boy, I managed to find a spot near him in the coach. His face was pale, gaunt, and he appeared vulnerable rather than aloof.

"How far are you going?" I asked, smiling. I knew I was taking a chance, so I quickly added, "I'm new here . . . I don't want to miss the Lexington Avenue stop."

"Oh, your stop comes well before mine," he said. "Don't worry. I'll let you know when to get off. I'm going to the World Trade Center, the last stop."

I racked my brains. I wanted to get some crucial information from him without arousing his suspicion. "Do you live in the Jackson Heights area?" I asked.

"Yes, but I'm moving out soon. In fact, all the tenants are moving out because my landlord wants to sell the house. Besides, I'm quitting my job. Today is my last day."

"Really? Where do you work?"

"At the World Trade Center," he said. "At a newsstand in the concourse. I also deliver newspapers and magazines to many of the offices."

We chatted about New York for a while. Then, saying that I was hoping to buy a house in Queens, I managed to get his address and phone number.

"I'm Satish," I said, as the train crossed over to Manhattan, giving us a spectacular view of the skyline. "Where are you from?"

"Atlanta." He shook my hand. "I'm Samir. Nice to meet you. Your stop is next."

Rushing to my office, breathless with excitement, I called Deepa. She volunteered to inform his family. Meanwhile, I told her, I'd look for the house and contact the landlord. We agreed that this delicate matter should be handled carefully, without alienating him.

On Sunday, the phone rang even before I was out of bed. It was Deepa. She said that Samir's mother, currently traveling, was very relieved and grateful to hear the news, but she wanted to speak to me. Deepa gave me her phone number. When I called the mother, she broke down and thanked me profusely for finding him. Samir had left home abruptly, she said, because he couldn't get along with his stepfather. Saying that she'd arrive in New York on Tuesday, she asked me to wait for her before going to the house. I offered to pick her up.

I took a day off from work. Since her flight was arriving in the afternoon, I didn't set the alarm and woke up later than usual. While shaving, I heard a commotion outside and somebody started banging on my front door. It was my neighbor in the building.

"Satish, did you hear the news?" Juan was gasping, as if something he'd swallowed was choking him. "There was an attack on the World Trade Center."

"What?" I said uncomprehendingly. "What do you mean?"

"Turn on the TV! They're saying that terrorists hijacked two planes and crashed them into the twin towers."

Stunned, I reached for the remote. Then, helplessly, I saw those horrifying images of death and destruction that seemed so unreal, as if we were watching a disaster film's apocalyptic scenes. I felt numb, sickened—and when I got up to get some water, my head spun, filling me with nausea. A woman was sobbing on the landing outside, as she talked on her phone, and through the window I could also hear the frightened, panic-stricken voices of the residents congregating downstairs. Maybe some of their loved ones worked there. I suddenly thought of Samir. Grabbing the cordless, I called the house number.

"Hello?" It was another tenant. The chaotic sounds from his TV echoed the sounds from my TV.

"Is Samir there?" I asked.

There was a pause. "No," he said. "He went to see his boss—"

"Boss?" My clammy hand gripped the phone. "Didn't he quit his job?"

"Yes, but today he went to collect money from his boss for overtime work."

Still feeling dizzy, I collapsed on the sofa. "Did he go to . . . Manhattan?"

"No, he went to his house. In Astoria, Queens. Who's calling?" He sounded a little annoyed.

I let out a big sigh. "One moment, please," I said, reaching for my glass of water.

HIDDEN LIVES

The sign in the commercial strip adjacent to a gas station, where Ashok had stopped to fill up his tank, was so incongruous that he decided to take a closer look. With just a couple of cars in the parking lot, the strip didn't look too prosperous, but it wasn't failing either and he saw signs for an insurance office and a travel agency—both closed—a hair salon that seemed empty, and a convenience store that was open. What really drew his attention, though, was the sign closest to the strip's entrance.

"Café Bhutan," it read in bright colors. Drawing nearer, Ashok saw a depiction of snow-capped mountains on a curtain in the window, enlivening a little what was otherwise a drab, anonymous building. The restaurant was closed, with no hours posted on the door, and Ashok was about to walk away when what appeared to be a red glow—visible through a gap in the curtain—stopped him. Stepping forward, he peered into what seemed like a small restaurant. On a counter close to the door, there was a cash register and a portable stove with a saucepan on it. A red flame flickered dangerously. Knocking loudly, he pushed on the door. It didn't budge, but he was startled to hear "Namaste."

The greeting, it took Ashok a moment to realize, came from behind him.

Turning around, he saw an indifferently dressed young woman smiling at him. Her faded green slacks had holes and the frilly white top was crumpled, making him wonder if she'd just gotten out of bed. Her dark hair was tied in a loose knot. But she was poised, even solicitous, and didn't seem annoyed by the intrusion.

"The restaurant is closed, sir . . . please come back later," she said, speaking with what sounded like the convent-educated accent he'd known as a boy.

"I was just checking. Isn't anybody here? The stove seems to be on."

That caught her off guard, and the smile vanished. Recovering quickly, she asked, "Are you from India, sir?"

Why was the girl jabbering? He said, impatiently, "Yes . . . do you know anything about this, miss? Seems dangerous. We may have to call 9-1-1."

"No, no, please don't do that, sir," she said in alarm, pointing at his phone. "I have the key. See. I went to Shop Now to get milk. See. I'm making some tea." Moving past him, she opened the door hastily and, turning to him, added, "Please come back later. The water is boiling . . . I'll turn off the stove." She slipped in and shut the door.

Returning to his car, Ashok drove to his client's office close by. Although not too familiar with the area, he knew there had been an influx of Bhutanese refugees in recent years to this section of the city. But until now he hadn't met a Bhutanese or, as far as he could tell, come across a Bhutanese-owned business. He wondered about the cuisine. Was it similar to Tibetan food, which he had eaten? What kind of discrimination had these refugees suffered in Bhutan, which loomed in his imagination only as a tranquil Shangri-La preoccupied with blissful Gross National Happiness, not grubby Gross National Product? And what sort of challenges did they face as new immigrants here? While he'd read about Tibet, the original Shangri-La, Ashok realized he knew little about Bhutan, which he'd long desired to visit. Even the name evoked a sense of mystery and longing. Speaking of mystery, was the girl a tenant at the restaurant, not just an employee? He'd also seen, through the gap in the curtain, a makeshift bed—a mattress, really—with a blanket and pillow on top, illuminated by a reading lamp on the floor. Was she sleeping there at night after working during the day?

That evening, instead of going from his office to Sunrise Apartments, where he now lived after his recent divorce, Ashok headed to Café Bhutan. Again, it didn't say if the restaurant was open or closed—but when he pushed the door and walked in, he saw a middle-aged couple dining quietly. Moments later, the young woman he'd seen that morning emerged from the kitchen, carrying two big dishes.

"Hello, sir," she said, smiling. "Good to see you again. Please have a seat. I'll be with you soon."

A pungent masala smell greeted Ashok, whetting his appetite and reminding him of Indian rather than any other cuisine. The décor was predictable but not disappointing, with *thangkas* and framed pictures of the Himalayas hanging on the walls. A smiling brass Buddha presided over the cash register, and a few potted plants occupied the corners. The portable stove was gone—and in the spot where he'd noticed the mattress and the lamp, he now saw a table and four chairs.

"I knew you'd be back," she said, handing him a menu. "I'm Mona. Let me know if you have questions. What's your name?"

"Ash-ok." He felt his cheeks burn, as his eyes remained focused on the menu. Taken aback, he wasn't sure if she was flirting with him. Maybe he was just confusing friendliness with flirtation. Still recovering from the abrupt dissolution of his marriage, he couldn't trust his judgement. He didn't want to do anything foolish. And the age difference? She seemed to be about a decade younger, though it was true that her small frame accentuated her girlish demeanor. Her English was impressive, and he wondered how she could have picked up that Anglicized accent in Bhutan. Obviously, she hadn't been in this country for long.

Apart from a chili-and-cheese stew called *Ema Datshi*, which was apparently Bhutan's national dish, and a minced chicken item (*Jasha Maroo*), the menu used a jumble of words—momos, samosas, jalfrezi, sekuwa, vindaloo, rogan josh, thupka, tandoori and tarkari—to list Nepali and Indian items. "I thought this was a Bhutanese restaurant," Ashok said when she returned to take his order.

"Well, it's Bin, not Bhut," Mona said, laughing. "It stands for 'Bhutanese-Indian-Nepali.' I just made that up. A Bhutanese of Nepali descent opened the restaurant, but now it's managed by an Indian who is also the chef. He changed the menu to attract more customers."

But the restaurant's name hadn't been changed, Ashok assumed, in order to keep Café Bhutan distinct from the bunch of Indian eateries that had sprung up in recent years. Having taken his order, Mona was walking towards the kitchen when the door leading to it swung open and an Indian man—presumably the chef—emerged, looking annoyed. He was good-looking in a rugged way, with a strong physique and deep-set, smoldering eyes that gave him the appearance of a wrestler more than a restaurateur. "*Jaldi*," he said brusquely and, continuing to speak in Hindi, asked Mona to come quickly to the kitchen and complete the task he'd assigned.

More than his manner, what surprised Ashok was the way she responded. Her feistiness gone, Mona answered meekly, in Hindi, and followed him to the kitchen. Was he more than just her boss? She became busier and less talkative, and Ashok also refrained from chatting with her, not wanting to create problems. Working for this man wasn't easy, apparently, or perhaps he was in a foul mood that day. Eating his food quickly, without enjoying it greatly, Ashok paid his bill. When he left a hefty tip, she smiled and said, "Thanks . . . please come again."

"I will." But he wasn't sure when—or if—he would return.

At his IT firm, as it turned out, Ashok got busy with a new project that involved travel. But about a month later, acting on an impulse, he made his way to the restaurant again. It was just to give the food another shot, he told himself, although this time he'd order something more familiar. Cooking had become a chore. But while he ate out regularly, his appetite for adventurous dining had diminished; what he seemed to crave was comfort food.

Eating out was something he and his ex-wife had enjoyed doing frequently in the early years of their marriage. It had started during their courtship, leading to the discovery of diverse cuisines in their teeming metro. And that triggered an interest in travel, which they enthusiastically pursued after getting married. Reveling in this shared interest, they gave no thought to having children. But then her attitude changed and what he'd understood to be a tacit agreement to remain childless fell apart. The glamor of overseas travel palled as her priorities shifted to, above all, having a baby.

Ashok resisted—selfishly, he realized—because he thought it would interfere with his plans. That led to quarrels, although their first quarrel was actually over the money they were spending on trips. One morning, waking up alone in the spare bedroom, he felt a stab in his chest. He wanted her beside him—and, yes, he wanted a child as well. But it was too late.

Entering Café Bhutan, Ashok was glad to see that Mona still worked there. She seemed a little distracted and distant. There were just a few customers, so it couldn't have been the workload. She greeted him pleasantly enough, but that earlier chattiness—perhaps even flirtation—was gone, replaced by a polite formality.

"Everything okay, Mona?" he said, as she handed him the menu.

"Yes, sir. How are you doing?"

"Fine, I guess. I'd have come earlier, but was out of town on business. My name is Ashok, by the way. Not sure if you remember."

She smiled. "Can I get you anything to drink?"

Ashok placed his order and, after she walked away, looked in the direction of the kitchen, wondering if the intimidating chef would emerge from there and bark at her. Mona did seem tense. Why did she continue working at Café Bhutan? Perhaps she had few options. It was an uneventful meal, although Ashok enjoyed it more this time, maybe because he had stuck to familiar dishes. Again, he left a big tip, which she didn't notice. But she spoke, surprising him with a request. "Ashok, can I see you outside briefly? I want to ask something. Please wait for me in your car. I'll be there soon."

He was dumbstruck. As Mona cleared the table, waiting for his answer without looking at him, the smile on her face seemed touched with anxiety.

"Of course, Mona," he said, finding his voice. "I'll wait for you."

"Thank you . . . it won't take long," she said, before walking away with the dishes.

The poorly lit parking lot was deserted and even the convenience store seemed closed. Café Bhutan was no longer officially open, and the other two diners had already left. Getting into his car, he wondered what it was she wanted to say. And why the secrecy? He got the answer soon when a car emerged from the back of the restaurant and, going past him, exited the parking lot. Though the light was dim, and the driver didn't look in his direction, Ashok caught a glimpse of him. It was the chef. Almost immediately, Mona, still in her waitressing outfit, came out of the restaurant and walked up to the car. "Sorry to bother you," she said, as he opened the door.

"No, no, it's not a problem at all, Mona. You want to sit? It's a little cool outside." She hesitated before slipping into the seat beside him. "What's on your mind?" he said, turning towards her.

"I'm looking for another job, but—"

"Yes?"

"I need some help," she said, lowering her head. "This is awkward . . . I shouldn't be delaying you like this."

"No, Mona, I'm in no rush. Maybe I can help."

"Well . . . I have immigration issues."

Feeling uncomfortable suddenly, Ashok wondered what he was getting into. Nevertheless, he said, "I know little about immigration matters, but we can check with an immigration attorney I know." He paused. "Did you come directly from Bhutan, Mona?"

"No, I'm not a refugee. And I'm not from Bhutan. I'm Indian."

"Really?" He was stunned. "I wouldn't have guessed it."

"Why, Ashok? Is it because I don't look like you?" Although the light was indistinct, he could see that she was smiling again.

"No, no, that's not what I meant," he said, flustered. "I said that because you work at what I thought was a Bhutanese restaurant." But she was right, in a way. Her features, with narrower eyes and a fairer complexion, had thrown him off. She'd reminded him of eastern Asia rather than the Indian subcontinent—and he was too embarrassed to admit it.

"That's okay. You wouldn't have known, anyway. It's a common mistake."

Well, that would explain the accent. She might have gone to a convent school in northeastern India. An incident, long-buried in his consciousness, came back to him. At his school in India, a new student—a boy who didn't look like the other children—joined his class one day, arousing curiosity. When he introduced himself (Ashok couldn't remember his name) and mentioned that he was from Arunachal Pradesh, somebody said, "Chinese." The class erupted in laughter. The teacher was so furious that she kept them indoors during recess. Soon, the boy blended in easily enough, but he left the school after a year, as Ashok recalled.

"Mona, you're from northeastern India, right?" he said. "From Meghalaya, perhaps?"

"Good guess! I'm from Manipur, actually. Imphal. But I did live in Meghalaya—and later moved to Delhi, where I worked at a hotel. That's where I met Hari. I came to America with him. He's our chef here. I think you saw him last time."

"Yes, I did. And I saw him tonight as he was leaving. So what happened? Things aren't going well?"

"It's complicated," she said, opening the door to leave. "I should have known better before getting involved with him. But it's late now."

Ashok wondered if she meant it was "too late now" to do anything about it. But no. She meant that it was time for her to get back to the restaurant and lock up.

Trying to fall asleep later that night, Ashok didn't know what he could do for Mona. It was a little baffling that she'd approached him. Perhaps she saw him as a fellow Indian who might be able to help her, or at least give some advice. As he knew from experience, immigrants who belonged to the same home country were more likely to look out for each other, even if they had little else in common. Did Mona, he wondered before drifting off, spend her nights at the restaurant because her relationship with Hari had soured and she had nowhere else to go?

The immigration attorney, returning Ashok's call late at night, said that he had an important case coming up soon. But he offered to see Mona the following day if they could come in the morning before he got busy. Rising early, Ashok drove to Café Bhutan and parked in the empty lot. Zipping up his jacket to ward off the chill, he walked over to the front door. She was in the restaurant, no doubt.

Ashok knocked, with trepidation. There was no response, so he knocked again—louder. A shuffling sound followed, and the curtain parted to reveal Mona's face. But when it closed quickly and she didn't respond for what seemed like several minutes, he wondered if he'd made a mistake. And then, just as he was about to walk away, she opened the door. She'd dressed hastily, but looked natty in a red top and jeans, as if she were a customer emerging from the restaurant, not an employee who'd just woken up. How did she mange to brush her hair so fast? The transformation was striking. Her expression, though, was solemn.

He spoke quickly. "My apologies for not giving you advance notice, Mona. The attorney said he'd offer a free consultation today if we can meet him in the morning."

She relaxed, and in her smile he saw the doubt change to hope. "Sure, that sounds good, Ashok. Thanks. I have a couple more hours. But can we chat first?"

They went to the Pancake House, a short distance away, in his car. As Ashok soon found out, Mona had first met Hari—he apparently preferred "Harry" these days—in Delhi, where she'd moved to with her sister from distant northeastern India. The sisters, with a friend's help, rented a room in a middle-class neighborhood, but then struggled to make a living, until Mona's sister became a secretary and Mona found a job at an upscale hotel that catered to the nouveau riche. Hari was already working there as a chef. He pursued Mona—and eventually, after initial reservations over his raffish reputation, she started a relationship with him. Then he persuaded her to accept his offer of a trip to America, where his brother lived. Balking at the expense, she was reluctant at first, though Hari said he'd pay for it. Her sister didn't trust him, and tried to dissuade Mona, saying that his intention to marry her meant nothing. But Mona believed him.

Only recently, after living in the States for months, did Mona realize her sister had been right. At first, Mona hadn't taken his plans seriously—but when, to her surprise, they both got U.S. visitor visas, there was no turning back. They quit their jobs at the hotel.

"Once we got here, things changed rapidly," Mona said, lowering her voice. "He has decided to stay . . . and seems to have found a way to do it. I'm not needed anymore."

"What happened?"

Mona was cautious, however. "Not here, Ashok. I have to get back to the restaurant."

"What about seeing the attorney?"

"Not now. We'll have to do it another time. Hari comes to the restaurant early sometimes. I don't want to take a chance."

Mona was nervous, and seemed to be having second thoughts about Ashok's offer. Not wanting to upset her, he remained silent as they walked back to the car. He wanted to ask why she hadn't left Hari, and why she was spending her nights at the restaurant.

"I've become an illegal alien, as they say here," she said, as if she'd read his mind. "My visa has expired."

So what went wrong? She smiled grimly. The money they'd brought from India dwindled rapidly, and they were broke in just a few weeks. Hari's brother, helpful at first, became aloof and seemed caught up in his own struggles. He was getting by rather than thriving, and the rosy reports he'd sent to India about his life in the States turned out to be overblown. But while Hari became disillusioned with his brother, he was excited about America, which did seem like the promised land to him. Being resourceful and gregarious, he had no trouble making contacts—and soon even found a job at a restaurant, where the only credential that mattered was the ability to make tasty dishes.

Mona was reluctant to enter this shadowy world of illegal employment, but the need for money—and Hari's pleas—made her take the plunge. She found a waitressing job. Still, she'd have left the country before her visa expired, avoiding any trouble, except that two unsettling discoveries—made within days last month—seemed to have upended her plans. Now she was in a quandary and didn't know what to do.

Having reached the commercial strip, Ashok was about to turn into the parking lot.

"Oh, my god, he's already here," Mona said, sounding frantic. "He'll explode if he finds out that I've been talking to you."

So Mona's apprehension wasn't misplaced—Hari was already at Café Bhutan. "Well, he doesn't have to know," Ashok said. "I'll drop you here. Tell him you went to the store."

Too late.

At the restaurant's entrance, Hari stood facing the parking lot. Was he looking for Mona? Perhaps he was wondering why she wasn't there. When Hari glanced at the car and saw Mona sitting inside, his face registered bewilderment, or shock, as if she were a ghost.

"Keep driving, please," Mona said. "He's going to be mad. I don't want a scene."

Ashok swerved, pulling away from the parking lot, and the car was back on the road, going straight. They remained silent for a few moments.

She spoke first. "Sorry to drag you into this mess, Ashok. But I cannot go back now."

"Don't worry about it, Mona. I'm sure things will get better soon."

"I don't know where to go. The restaurant became my home about a month ago when I found out he was having an affair. The woman is a U.S. citizen, and he intends to marry her. It was a calculated move, I realized. She is his one-way ticket to America. I'm glad, in a way, except . . . " Her voice broke and trailed off. She looked away.

"It's okay, Mona . . . we'll deal with it," he said, feeling awkward and struggling to find the right words. Was he drawn to her? No doubt. But it was more than that, he was sure. Wasn't it time for him to live less selfishly?

"Except," she continued, "I found out in the same week that I was pregnant. I chose not to tell him. It's all for the best."

Ashok almost caused an accident, but quickly regaining his composure, he turned towards Sunrise Apartments—which they'd reached by now—and entered the complex. It didn't take long to park in front of his building. She sat quietly, staring ahead.

"You can stay here, Mona . . . in fact, I want you to stay," he said, removing his key from the ignition. "It's an apartment, but I have enough room. It can be your home."

Mona didn't say anything, but she looked at him and smiled wanly.

BRAHMS IN THE LAND OF BRAHMA

"Steve . . . Steve . . . how are you? Do you know who I am?"

"Narayan."

"Very good. And the music?"

"Brahms. Fourth symphony, third movement."

"Excellent, Steve! I knew you'd be okay. The doctor will be here soon. Don't worry. Everything is under control. Hope to take you home soon."

Narayan's glasses, as he leaned forward, slipped down his nose, and from his brow, before he fished out a handkerchief and mopped it, glistening beads of perspiration threatened to fall on the hospital bed. He must have been drinking hot chai. Every morning at Narayan's home, Steve would see him reach for the fan switch as soon as chai was served. Then, after handing Steve the *Express of India*, he'd sit back and read the local vernacular paper, while they waited for scrambled eggs and buttered toast—or, less frequently, fluffy idlis and crispy dosas with chutney and sambhar.

Why was he listening to Brahms—*his* CD, surely?—and how long had he been lying there? The lively third movement having followed the lovely second movement, now came the Bach-inspired, ingeniously weaving melody of the final movement—his favorite—and as Steve lay still, listening, the familiar music swelled majestically.

"Your CD, my player," Narayan said, smiling, as if he'd read Steve's mind. Clad in a white, loose-fitting khadi shirt, and sporting bushy eyebrows and longish grey hair, he looked like a benign swami who was about to bestow his blessings. "The hospital was okay with it, Steve. Music is a healer, no? Isn't Brahms a great composer?"

Tired and a little annoyed, Steve turned away. Why these questions? And why this pretence that he'd be going back to Narayan's house, since Steve had already given his notice and was going to check into a hotel? While there was little pain, he was still groggy—it was the drugs, no doubt—and he didn't feel like talking. Feeling constricted, he wished he could drift off again. He closed his eyes and tried to sleep, but then remembering something, he opened them and saw Narayan peering at him, still smiling.

"Mahesh . . . what happened to the driver?"

"Mahesh will be fine," Narayan said, patting his shoulder. "Don't worry, Steve. He was also wearing his seatbelt, thanks to you."

If it hadn't been for his friend Rupa, who lived on the same street back in the U.S., Steve would have checked into a hotel in India—where the company he worked for was based—just as he'd done on his first visit. But when Rupa told him about Narayan, whom she knew and offered to call on his behalf, Steve decided to be a paying guest at an Indian home this time, not only because the idea appealed to him but because he knew it would be more economical and maybe more interesting than staying in a hotel. Narayan lived not far from Info Tech City, where Steve would be working. Now that he was an independent IT consultant, he'd have to be careful with his money until he could establish himself.

After a couple of phone chats with Narayan, Steve arrived in India and moved into his house the same day. At the last minute, Narayan had unexpectedly sweetened the deal by offering his car for Steve's use—and so, it was Narayan's driver, Mahesh, who came to the airport to pick him up, holding a sign that read "Mr. STEVE of USA."

"Good morning," Narayan said when Steve, bleary-eyed, emerged from his room the following day. "Our chai is ready, Steve. Would you like to see today's paper?"

Steve wasn't keen on it right then, but as he sat on the brown sofa facing Narayan, he politely took the newspaper from him and glanced at the first page. "Gridlock in Parliament," a headline announced. He felt a sense of déjà vu and wondered, fleetingly, why it didn't say "Congress," only to realize that he was looking at the *Express of India.*

"Steve, I wanted to say something." Narayan folded his vernacular paper and took a steaming cup from his housekeeper. "I know you're not married, but if your girlfriend wants to visit, she's welcome to stay here. I'm not as conservative as I may seem to you."

Steve smiled, and sipped his chai. He'd already sensed that, as a host, Narayan, who was retired and had never married, would be sociable and voluble, giving him less privacy than he was accustomed to. But that didn't worry Steve, because Narayan's manner, far from being intrusive, made him feel welcome and less lonely than he'd been for over five months, following the abrupt—and painful—end of his last relationship.

Steve said he was single—and, no, he wasn't expecting any visitors from the States.

"You're single, Steve? Well, who knows, you may end up with a wife here—or, as we say, bibi. I run an unofficial matchmaking service; it's called Hurry-and-Marry." Narayan laughed, his belly shaking.

An explosion interrupted their conversation, just as Steve drained his cup. Startled, he stood up and, through the open balcony door, spotted a plume of white smoke in the distance curling into what seemed like a question mark.

"Not to worry," Narayan said, unperturbed. "It's only the military doing their testing. Come, Steve, I'll show you."

Standing on the balcony, Steve was surprised to see a vast expanse of uninhabited, wooded land that he hadn't noticed earlier. The government-owned property hadn't been gobbled up by developers, thank god, Narayan said, and the occasional noise of bomb testing, which rattled the windows, was a price worth paying, because no other place outside the few remaining parks in this booming yet congested city had such a luxurious stretch of greenery, making you feel—at least when you looked on this side—that you were in the tranquil countryside, far from the chaos and clamor of urban India.

"Now *this* boom is a boon for us," Narayan added, with his belly laugh.

The metro area had grown rapidly in the last several years as a result of the IT revolution, attracting droves of domestic migrants and transients, along with a growing number of foreign residents. Steve, though, still felt like a visitor, a stranger. Turning left, he got a partial view of Info Tech City's gleaming towers, where the ambiance was ultramodern and the working conditions so efficient—with power, clean water and hot food available 24/7—that Steve felt he was back at his old job, albeit in a tropical setting.

It was a tale of two cities. These islands of calm, familiar to Steve because of his work, were surrounded by the metro's surging waves of humanity, which had come as a shock to his system on his first visit. He'd never seen so many people massed in one place. But now, standing on the balcony, Steve felt as if he'd swigged a bracing tonic, a tonic he knew he could handle in moderate doses. The vast country was fascinating yet bewildering, stimulating but also overwhelming.

Turning right and looking past the alley humming with activity, Steve caught a glimpse of the haze-shrouded main road, which he knew would soon be crowded with pedestrians and a mix of vehicles, not to mention the odd cow ambling near the busy vegetable market. Shops would be opening presently, and roadside vendors would be doing brisk business.

When Steve thought of India, he pictured himself sitting in a jasmine-scented garden, where the chirping of birds mingled agreeably with the strains of a sitar—only to clash with the constant blaring of horns outside. India was contradictory; it was both modern and ancient, with the 21st century co-existing, easily and uneasily, with earlier centuries.

And everything seemed more intense. The sun was sharper, the colors brighter, the sounds harsher, the smells stronger, the pollution greater, the air warmer, the rains heavier, the food spicier, the chai sweeter, and the fruits tastier. Even the television dramas, or melodramas, Narayan watched were louder, unfolding at a higher emotional pitch than Steve was used to, going by what he'd observed the previous evening.

"Come, Steve, let's have breakfast," Narayan said, placing his hand on his back.

For earlier generations of American travelers, Steve liked to say when anybody back home asked him about India, the attraction lay in spiritual traditions. For him, it was software solutions. Steve would laugh, but he was only half-joking, because it was true that most of his time—and energy—was spent in Info Tech City, where he sat before a computer screen in a posh office, or interacted with clients and attended to their needs.

Wanting it to be a little different this time, Steve was glad he'd accepted Rupa's recommendation. Narayan, who frequently wore immaculate white clothes that included a dhoti wrapped around his waist and reaching his ankles, was steeped in his country's dominant cultural traditions, judging by his well-appointed home, which was adorned with framed pictures of various gods and goddesses, brass sculptures of elephants and a dancing Nataraja, and paintings depicting classical dancers, temples and sacred rivers, and picturesque village scenes.

And then there was the puja room where Narayan prayed every morning after his shower. Steve, not particularly religious, was intrigued by Narayan's deep yet unshowy piousness. It was obvious in the devotional music he enjoyed listening to, the clothes he wore at home, the vegetarian food he always ate, the incense sticks he lit before his puja every day, filling the room with a pleasing fragrance.

Steve saw at first hand what he had, until then, only vaguely known—culture in India was often inextricably tied to its religious traditions. This was apparent even in prime-time television serials, some of which were based on mythological characters from the epics.

Then, of course, there was the newer and younger and more secular India that Steve already knew about and which he began to experience again in Info Tech City, where he worked alongside ambitious, often Westernized Indians in up-to-date office buildings. Narayan's house was also a welcoming island in the pullulating metro, though of a different sort, and at the end of a long and tiring day, after riding in Narayan's car on the choked highway leading out of Info Tech City, Steve was glad to be back. Mahesh, a competent driver, was accommodating no matter when Steve wanted to leave. But he seemed to think his seatbelt was a luxury—or a hindrance—that he could push aside before starting the car, making Steve nervous. He decided to speak to Mahesh about it, gently.

"What were you listening to, Steve? Yesterday."

"Excuse me?"

They were having dinner, which Narayan's housekeeper, Shanti, had prepared and was now serving. Although Steve hadn't made any requests, she made sure there was one nonvegetarian dish for him at every meal; this time it was a delectably tangy fish curry.

Shanti, a widow belonging to a different community than Narayan's, lived with her daughter and son-in-law close by. She came to the house in the morning and left only after they'd eaten in the evening. Her attachment to Narayan was striking—and yet, Steve couldn't help being aware of the distance between them, dictated by social circumstances that perhaps remained unbridgeable. Always deferential, she never ate in their presence, preferring to eat alone in the kitchen after they were done and she'd cleared the table.

"I heard this beautiful music coming from your room last night," Narayan said. "I wanted to ask you about it, but your door was closed. I didn't want to disturb you."

"Oh, you're welcome to knock anytime, Narayan. Yesterday? I was listening to Brahms—"

"How wonderful! Reminds me of Brahma."

"I'm sorry . . . who?"

"Brahma, Steve. He's the creator of the universe for Hindus. But Brahma is less well known than the other two in the trinity: Vishnu, the preserver, and Shiva, the destroyer."

After they finished eating, Narayan took Steve to the puja room and showed him a bronze idol of the multiheaded Brahma, resting on a makeshift altar and surrounded by other deities in the pantheon. Narayan said he was a devotee of Brahma, though India had just a few well-known temples dedicated to Brahma. "And you're a devotee of Brahms, so maybe it was fate that brought us together," he added, chuckling.

"I don't know about devotee," Steve said, "but it's true that, lately, I've been listening to Brahms a lot."

"I can see why. The music you were playing was divine. I'd like to listen more, Steve, if you don't mind. I'm ignorant about Western music—of any kind."

"Certainly, Narayan. You're welcome to take my CDs anytime. Perhaps we can listen together sometimes. And I'm hoping you can tell me more about Indian music."

Less than a week later, this pleasant cross-cultural engagement, as Steve saw it, ended abruptly. When Steve got back from work, Narayan would usually greet him brightly and, turning to his housekeeper, say: "Shanti, make chai. Steve is here."

But that evening, returning home, Steve didn't see Narayan and mistakenly thought he'd stepped out. As he was finishing his chai, a glum-looking Narayan emerged from his room and said, "Mr. Steve, I want to speak to you about something."

"Is everything okay, Narayan?"

"I don't know. This morning, after you left, I noticed that you'd accepted my friend request on Facebook."

"Yes?" Steve had been surprised to receive the request, not having seen Narayan use his computer or even his smartphone.

"Steve, I hope you don't think I'm nosy. I was browsing through your album and saw some nice photos of your life in America. I was just curious.

Then I saw one that showed you . . . and Tom." His voice dropped. "I had no idea . . . Rupa never told me."

Steve bristled. "Told you what, Narayan? You're welcome to look at my pictures, but I don't see why my personal life should be any of your business. Tom and I are no longer together, but that's irrelevant."

"Sorry, Steve . . . I'm old-fashioned. Please don't misunderstand me. It's my mistake."

"Well, seems like we both made a mistake." Steve said, rising. "I'm so disappointed, Narayan." Walking quickly to his room, he closed the door.

He felt a little agitated. Sitting on the bed, he distractedly reached for his stack of CDs.

The opening section of the Brahms Piano Quintet, with its seductive blend of strings and piano, unfolded at a low volume as Steve pondered his next move. A hotel in Info Tech City, where he'd stayed last time, would cost a lot more, but that seemed like his best bet for the short term. Looking for his notebook, in which he'd jotted down local hotel phone numbers and other information, Steve noticed that his camera, which he remembered leaving on the window sill after taking pictures around the house a few days earlier, was missing. It was an expensive new model, and Steve had it only because his brother had given it to him as a gift. He searched the room thoroughly, without luck, and wondered if he was losing his mind. Could he have taken it to the office and left it there?

Not long after the quintet ended with a thrilling flourish, Shanti knocked on the door and said softly, "Dinner, Mr. Steve."

Steve and Narayan ate quietly as Shanti served them and, like she often did, shuttled between the dining area and kitchen, bringing fresh rotis, roasted poppadams or filtered water. At the end came a milky, sweet-smelling vermicelli pudding that Steve had never had before.

Thanking Shanti for the delicious meal, Steve asked her, after she took his plate, if she'd come across his camera when she was cleaning the room. As usual, Shanti, understanding only a few words of what Steve said—their rudimentary communication involved a lot of smiles and gestures—turned to Narayan for translation.

"What do you mean?" Narayan said, putting his spoon down. "Why would she touch your camera? She's trustworthy."

"That's not what I said, Narayan." Steve felt his anger rise. "You're being impossible. All I wanted to know was if she'd seen the camera. I'm merely trying to find it, in case I misplaced it. But, you know what, it doesn't matter."

"Steve, don't get upset. Please. Did you look everywhere . . . ?"

Steve had, however, already got up from his chair and was walking away. Entering his room, he shut the door firmly.

After Steve was discharged from the hospital, he didn't object when Narayan took him back to his house to recuperate. A hotel seemed out of the question, at least for now.

Besides, Narayan insisted, saying, "You're my responsibility, Steve, until you make a full recovery."

Earlier, a day after that unpleasant exchange of words at the dining table, Steve had given his notice and also mentioned that he'd switch to a cab service for his daily commute.

"Let's talk about it," Narayan said, sounding distressed. "I'm sorry, Steve. I know you felt insulted. That wasn't my intention."

"Not *insulted*, Narayan; *hurt* would be more appropriate. But I know you didn't mean it, and I'm sorry as well. Still, I think it would be better if I move on."

Narayan accepted Steve's decision, but he persuaded him to stick with his car and driver for the time being. Steve had to visit a couple of clients that day, so he went with Mahesh to the city. As they drove back in the evening traffic, it rained heavily, making the roads slick. A bus was making a turn when it skidded and hit Narayan's car from behind. It happened so fast that all Steve could remember was the sound of crunching metal and shattering glass. Neither Mahesh nor Steve had life-threatening injuries, but the medical expenses still added up alarmingly. The bus company, accepting responsibility, agreed to cover them fully.

"Ah, Steve, I see that you have a book about Kerala," Narayan said, as he walked into his room, holding a cup of chai and the *Express of India*. "No Brahms today?"

"Well, I'm giving him a break, I guess." Steve was partially reclining on the bed, with a few pillows to prop up his back. Putting his book down, he took the cup. "Thanks, Narayan. I'm still hoping to visit Kerala later this year."

"I'm sure you will, Steve. You're already making good progress." He paused. "I'm so glad we found the camera. Hope it wasn't damaged."

The camera had been lying on the ledge just outside the window. Presumably, a bird had dropped it there—or more likely, pushed it from the sill.

Steve held up his hand. "No worries, Narayan. I'd been foolish to leave it here, and then make a fuss. The camera is not important, but I won't use the open window as a shelf from now on."

Narayan smiled, and Steve was glad that there was no lingering awkwardness.

"By the way," Narayan said, "Kerala has one of the few notable Brahma temples in India. We plan to visit Kerala, too, after we get married."

Steve put his cup down. "You're getting married, Narayan? This is news to me."

Narayan looked away, and then down, before smiling at Steve. "I know," he said. "It was a sudden decision. I'm still in shock. Shanti and I have decided to get married."

Quietly, Steve gazed at him. Like India, he realized, Narayan could be full of surprises.

ACKNOWLEDGMENTS

My gratitude and appreciation to Heather and Charles, not to mention the other wonderful members of the Wising Up TEAM, for their trust, encouragement, assistance, and mastery. I couldn't have asked for better readers or more caring editors. I also want to thank my family and dear colleagues at *Khabar* magazine for their unstinting support and camaraderie.

The stories in this collection, or different versions of the stories included here, first appeared in the following publications:

Ashes – *Rosebud.*

Interview with the World's Oldest Man, **Indian Uncle Sam**, **Holi Day in America** and **The Last Stop** – *India Abroad.*

Do You Remember? – *The Wagon Magazine.*

Where the Grass Is Greener and **Fragments of Glass** – *India Currents.*

In the New World – *Crossing Class: The Invisible Wall* (Wising Up Press).

The Missing Husband – *South Asian Review.*

The Visitor and the Neighbor – *AIM: America's Intercultural Magazine*

River of Silence and **Brahms in the Land of Brahma** – *Lakeview International Journal of Literature of Arts.*

Memories of Mission Valley – *The Missing Slate.*

Anil's Visit – *Smoky Blue Literary and Arts Magazine.*

What Sid Knew – *Scarlet Leaf Review.*

Migrant – *The Apple Valley Review.*

The Plot – *Strands Lit Sphere.*

Hidden Lives – *Muse India.*

AUTHOR

Murali Kamma is the managing editor of *Khabar*, a monthly magazine catering to the Indian-American community in the Southeast. While he did dabble in fiction as a youth (a few early stories appeared in an Indian magazine), it was his life as an immigrant straddling two cultures—and his work as an editor—that inspired him to pursue it more seriously. After graduating from Loyola College in India, he continued his education at the State University of New York at Buffalo. His stories have appeared in numerous journals, including *Rosebud, South Asian Review,* and *Lakeview International Journal of Literature and Arts.* He has enjoyed interviewing, among other authors, Salman Rushdie, Anita Desai, William Dalrymple, Chitra Banerjee, Divakaruni, and Pico Iyer. A naturalized U.S. citizen, he lives with his family in Atlanta.

IMMIGRATION, CITIZENSHIP & BELONGING

from Wising Up Press

GREEN CARD
& OTHER ESSAYS
Áine Greaney

COMPLEX ALLEGIANCES
Constellations of Immigration, Citizenship & Belonging
A Wising Up Anthology

SHIFTING BALANCE SHEETS:
Women's Stories of Naturalized Citizenship & Acculturation
A Wising Up Anthology

THE 2018 IMMIGRATION DEBATE:
Trump Faces Public Opinion
(ebook)
Charles D. Brockett

VISIT OUR BOOKSTORE: www.universaltable.org

WISING UP PRESS COLLECTIVE

Fiction

Only Beautiful & Other Stories
Live Your Life & Other Stories
My Name Is Your Name & Other Stories
Kerry Langan

Germs of Truth: Stories about families of all ages, stages, orientations—and sperm banks
The Philosophical Transactions of Maria van Leeuwenhoek
Heather Tosteson

Memoirs

Journeys with a Thousand Heroes: A Child Oncologist's Story
John Graham-Pole

Keys to the Kingdom: Reflections on Music and the Mind
Kathleen L. Housley

Last Flight Out: Living, Loving & Leaving
Phyllis A. Langton

Poetry

Breathing in Portuguese, Living in English
Heather Tosteson

A Hymn that Meanders
Maria Nazos

Epiphanies
Kathleen L. Housley

WISING UP ANTHOLOGIES

CROSSING CLASS: *The Invisible Wall*

SURPRISED BY JOY

THE KINDNESS OF STRANGERS

SIBLINGS: *Our First Macrocosm*

CREATIVITY & CONSTRAINT

CONNECTED: *What Remains as We All Change?*

DARING TO REPAIR: *What Is It, Who Does It & Why?*

VIEW FROM THE BED, VIEW FROM THE BEDSIDE

DOUBLE LIVES, REINVENTION & THOSE WE LEAVE BEHIND

LOVE AFTER 70

FAMILIES: *The Frontline of Pluralism*

ILLNESS & GRACE, TERROR & TRANSFORMATION

CPSIA information can be obtained
at www.ICGtesting.com
Printed in the USA
FSHW021507120619
58934FS

9 781732 451438